The Seeker Siblings

The Siblings' Double Troubles

Andrew Powers

If you purchased this book without a cover, you should be aware that this book is stolen property. It was reported as "unsold and destroyed" to the publisher, and neither the author nor the publisher has received any payment for this "stripped" book.

No part of this book may be reproduced in whole or in part, or stored in a retrieval system, or transmitted in any form or by any means, electronic, mechanical, photocopying, recording, or otherwise, without written permission from the author. For more information regarding permissions, contact Andrew Powers. City of Publication: Oakdale, Minnesota.

ISBN 978-1-962266-00-0 (pbk.)

Library of Congress Control Number: 2023919963

This is a work of fiction. Unless otherwise indicated, all the names, characters, businesses, places, events, and incidents in this book are either the product of the author's imagination or used in a fictitious manner. Any resemblance to actual events, locations, or persons, living or dead, is purely and entirely coincidental.

Text copyright © 2023 by Andrew Powers.
All rights reserved.

To my mother, Amy.

The mom who supports my dreams,
risks everything, and loves endlessly.

CONTENTS

	Prologue: A New Adventure	1
1.	The Seeker Siblings	10
2.	The Second Siblings	19
3.	Puzzling Playground Problems	28
4.	Discussions	39
5.	Astro's Investigation	53
6.	Astra's Investigation	62
7.	Switch Siblings	74
8.	The Vivid Visions	87
9.	Paving the Plans	103
10.	The Missing Information	112
11.	The Program Before School	124
12.	Two Truths and a Lie	141
13.	Friends and Families	155

The Seeker Siblings

The Siblings' Double Troubles

— PROLOGUE —

A New Adventure

Slumping in their car seats as lunch crawls closer, the Seeker family grows peckish and irritable as their stomachs growl for food. After riding in the car for several hours, their bodies beg for a good stretch.

"Dear," says Mrs. Seeker, sitting in the passenger's seat. "Let's get off at the next exit for some food."

Mr. Seeker's stomach growls at him. "Looks like my stomach agrees," he says with a chuckle. "But it'll be a few minutes until the next exit."

Mrs. Seeker grins, shifts in her seat, and looks at her children in the back. "Maybe we'll be able to find a fast-food restaurant with a playground."

Astra squeals. "Let's play a game until then! Oo! Like the alphabet memory game!"

"Okay," Mrs. Seeker accepts, looking to the other seat. "Astro? Did you want to play?"

"C-Can I use my notebook to write down the order?"

"What? NO!" Astra objects. "That's not even a game! You're supposed to try and *memorize* the order! That's how it works!"

Astro huffs. "*Okay,* but you two are better at that, so I should get some help!"

"*Noo!* 'Cause then you'd win since you don't have to memorize anyth —"

"Okay, okay, calm down," says Mrs. Seeker, trying to extinguish the growing fire. "Why don't we play word chain instead?"

"What?" Astra complains. "But I thought we were going to play —"

"Oop!" Mr. Seeker interrupts, pulling into a fast-food parking lot. "Too late." He parks the car, opens the door, and steps out.

Astra sighs and drops her shoulders. "Okay, after!" she exclaims. "Let's play after!"

"Let's just focus on eating lunch," Mrs. Seeker says, opening her door and stepping out with her husband.

Astro and Astra grumble at each other as they follow their parents across the parking lot and into the restaurant.

Filling their stomachs and replenishing their energy levels, they swallow their remaining bites of food. After,

★ THE SIBLINGS' DOUBLE TROUBLES ★

Astro and Astra rush to the indoor playground tubes and start a game of hide-and-seek tag.

Crawling to find the best hiding spot, Astra stumbles upon a sobbing little girl. Starting to turn around, Astra unintentionally puts herself in the small girl's shoes. She feels every sob sink into her bones, and her heart drops. Tears collect in her eyes, and her stomach starts hurting as she senses the girl's feelings of helplessness. She looks away and blinks rapidly to dry her eyes. Abandoning her search for the perfect hiding spot, Astra feels a rush of adrenaline pump into her veins.

Cranking her charm levels to the max, Astra playfully slides over to the weeping girl. "Oh nyo!" she says, using a silly tone. "Why are you crying? My name's Astra. What's yours?"

The girl sniffles and wipes her tears. Through her whimpers and hiccups, she stutters, "H-H-Haley. I can't find m-my —"

"FOUND YOU!" Astro shouts, tagging Astra on the back.

Haley jumps from Astro's shouting, and tears begin rolling down her cheeks again.

Astra exhales and turns around, shooting him an unamused expression. "Astroo," she scolds.

"Woah, what? What'd I do?"

Astra turns back to Haley. "I'm sorry," she says with a soft voice and an even softer expression — to calm the girl down. "This is my brother. I know he *looks* scary, but he's nice . . . usually."

Astro returns Astra's unamused expression to the back of her head before looking at Haley. "H-Hello," he greets with a bashful tone. "W-Why are you crying?"

"I-I can't find my brother."

"Hm? Oh. Well, I just passed someone who looked a bit . . . lost."

"What? That's great!" cheers Astra, glancing between Astro and Haley. "Maybe it's your brother. So" — looking into Astro's eyes — "which way was he heading?"

Astro stares blankly. "Uhh . . ."

Astra squints and jerks her head to the side. "Astro, *really?* You just passed —"

"Well, I'm sorry!" he shouts. "I didn't realize I was supposed to keep track of every single person in . . . this . . ." Astro's voice trails off as Haley begins tearing up again.

"Astro," whispers Astra.

He sighs. "Okay, just shh," he hushes before closing his eyes.

★ THE SIBLINGS' DOUBLE TROUBLES ★

Astra smiles and puts her finger against her lips, encouraging Haley to be quiet.

After a minute, Astro opens his eyes. "Okay. I think he's heading up to the top. So if we go up to the swirly slide, we should run into the boy I saw."

"Shall we?" Astra asks.

Haley nods and follows the Seeker siblings through the different tubes. Soon, they reach the top level and crawl toward the slide.

Upon their arrival, they hear a boy shout, "HALEY!"

"DUSTIN!" cries Haley, rushing over to hug him.

While Haley and Dustin collect themselves, Astro's eyes begin to ache. He lightly tugs on Astra's shirt, leans toward her ear, and whispers, "W-We should go."

Feeling her adrenaline wearing off, Astra yawns and nods.

Haley and Dustin ride the swirly slide and pop out at the bottom. The Seeker siblings follow them.

After saying their goodbyes, Astro and Astra rejoin their parents and exit the restaurant. Hopping into their car, they continue their road trip.

Several minutes later, Astro's head pounds. "Mom!" he cries, holding his head between his hands. "W-Will you give me part of a pill?"

★ THE SEEKER SIBLINGS ★

Mrs. Seeker whips her head around, rapidly glancing between her children. "What happened?" she questions, seeing Astra falling asleep beside him. Simultaneously, she uses her right hand to open the glove compartment and grab a prescription bottle.

Astro winces and whispers, "Helped . . . crying girl." He holds his hand out and receives a partial pill from his mother.

Astro grabs a nearby water bottle and takes a drink to help him swallow his medicine. Using a blanket, he shields his eyes from the intense sunlight. After a few minutes, he falls asleep beside Astra.

With their children asleep, Mr. Seeker peeks over at Mrs. Seeker. "It's alright, sweetie. They'll be okay," he reassures, noticing his wife staring at their kids. He adds, "Luckily, the doctors found a medicine that helps his migraines. Huh?"

Mrs. Seeker continues watching over their children — who are both out of commission. "Yeah," she says with a gentle smile. "Thankfully."

Over an hour later, the Seeker twins wake up from their nap.

★ THE SIBLINGS' DOUBLE TROUBLES ★

"Hey," says Mr. Seeker. "Your mom and I have been talking . . . and we think it's a good idea to try and lay low for a little bit."

"Lay low?" repeats Astro.

"Mh-hmm, right," Mr. Seeker says. "Remember how everyone kept showing up at our house asking for help? We realize you two enjoy solving mysteries and helping people, but I think —"

"Wait!" Astra interrupts. "You're saying not to help people?"

Mrs. Seeker raises her head. "No, no! That's not what we're saying," she answers. "We realize that's what it might sound like, but that's not quite it." She stops and thinks.

A few minutes pass before Mr. Seeker jumps back into the conversation. "Astra," he says, adjusting the rear-view mirror to look at his daughter. "Remember how exhausted you got when you tried helping everyone who showed up at our house?"

"Pft, no! What? I was *fine!* I wasn't even . . ." Astra notices her family's expressions and senses their doubts. "I-I mean . . . w-well I . . . yeah."

★ THE SEEKER SIBLINGS ★

"Mh-hmm," Mr. Seeker hums sympathetically, "and we all know that Astro isn't a huge fan of the spotlight, right?"

Astra peeks at Astro — who is busy turning red and staring out his window. "Yeah," she says, taking his feelings into consideration. "O-Okay . . . then what do you want us to do?"

"We don't want you to stop helping people," says Mrs. Seeker. "But please . . . do so cautiously."

Mr. Seeker nods along. "We just don't want you two feeling trapped into helping everyone because they have a problem. So if you lend your help, do so with judgment."

"And don't be afraid to say no," adds Mrs. Seeker. "Okay?"

The twins nod, and several moments of silence pass.

Eventually, Mr. Seeker adjusts the mirror to include both of his children. "Astro. Astra," he says with a stern voice. "We want you both safe. And we want you to feel safe at our new house. So, if you're going to help people, please do so with caution. Does that make sense?"

Astro squints and furrows his eyebrows. "So, help people . . . but be careful about saying too much?"

★ THE SIBLINGS' DOUBLE TROUBLES ★

"Right," Mr. Seeker says, looking over at his daughter. "Astra?"

"Y-Yeah . . . I think so," she answers. "So, we should be careful about who we help."

The siblings sit with worried expressions as they think about their parents' request.

Mrs. Seeker senses their worry. "Please don't forget that we'll always be looking out for you," she comforts. "So if things end up . . . poorly, we'll deal with it as a family. There's no need to worry!"

Mr. Seeker smiles. "And don't forget how much we love you!" he emphasizes. "Just . . . remember to be kids. Y'know, make friends, have fun, all that good stuff."

The twins smile and nod before beginning a movie. They rest their heads on their neck pillows and fall back asleep.

— CHAPTER ONE —

The Seeker Siblings

The Seeker siblings frequently found themselves being stared at by strangers in amazement, fear, and sometimes both. From an early age, they realized their unique hair and distinct eyes caught people's attention whether they liked it or not. And with one look, you'd know that these twins were not your ordinary pair of siblings. Whether it was their genetics, parents' stories, or experiments and experiences, the twins discovered they had several unique talents.

Astro learned he could paint vivid scenarios inside his head; the more information he had, the better the vision. Astra realized she could take brief recordings of her memories and recall them temporarily before they became regular memories.

Strolling into their new school in their new town, in their new state, the Seeker siblings see students turning and staring.

★ THE SIBLINGS' DOUBLE TROUBLES ★

Astro walks meekly but with a firm and unwavering stance. He's cautious and prepared to react to anything that may happen. Even though the small, skinny boy creates a shy aura, his sharp eyes give another impression. His intense gaze often intimidates and, at times, frightens his peers. With this unique combination of traits, Astro is a walking enigma.

Astra sways and bounces on the balls of her feet beside him. Widening her eyes while flashing a cheeky smile, she spins and twirls down the halls. Thriving on attention, Astra uses her charisma and charm to draw people's gazes toward herself and away from Astro.

If either twin captivates you enough to look, there's a good chance one — if not both — is glancing back.

Astro shifts his piercing gaze toward Astra. "You look fidgety today," he says, tracking her with his eyes.

"Wrong!" she teases, finishing a twirl to look at him. "But *you* seem just as nervous as always."

He opens his mouth to deny it but pauses and lets out a quick, quiet huff. "What was the teacher's name again?" he asks, switching the subject.

Loosely shaking her head, Astra says, "You and that memory. Don't worry! I swear" — quickly peeking at the nearby classroom — "I'm paying attention!"

★ THE SEEKER SIBLINGS ★

Eventually, the siblings arrive at a classroom with inspirational quotes taped to the open door.

Astra stops and looks at the nameplate above the doorway. "Here *she* is," she says with a grin.

Astro stares at the row of hanging backpacks and the decorated door. "Hmph."

Walking to the end of the built-in coatrack, Astro and Astra hang their bags on the available hooks.

Even though materials are being provided by their classroom — basic supplies for new students — the Seeker siblings retrieve several items from their bags. Astra grabs a folder, a matching spiral-bound notebook, and a pencil. Astro retrieves his special hard-covered notebook. Afterward, they close their backpack and walk to the open door.

Woo! Woo! Woo! Woo! The bell chimes as they enter their new fifth-grade classroom.

★ THE SIBLINGS' DOUBLE TROUBLES ★

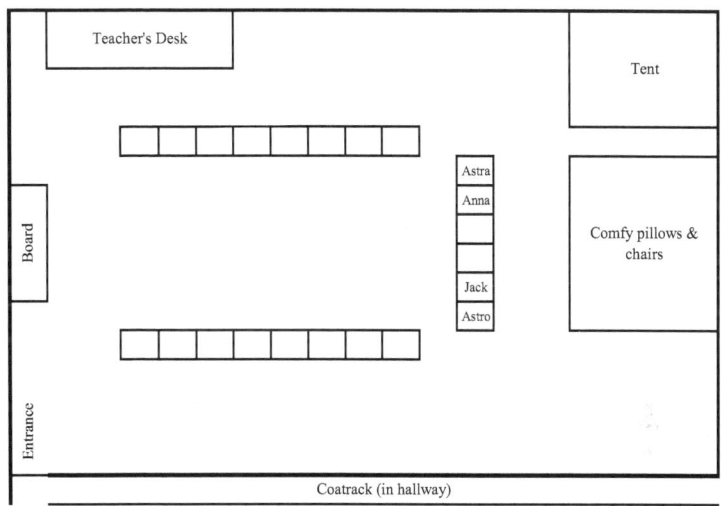

Ignoring the students, the siblings swiftly scan the room. Identifying the same items, Astro and Astra have a similar thought process. *We enter on the side. Board is in the front. The teacher's desk is across from the door. U-shaped desk arrangement. A gap in the middle of the room. A comfy space near the back, and — What in the world! Is that a tent in the corner?*

"Good morning!" greets a boisterous woman from across the room. A lady with dark-brown hair leaps up from her desk chair. Sidestepping her desk, she rushes to the door and approaches the siblings with an enormous smile. "My name's Ms. White! Considering I haven't

★ THE SEEKER SIBLINGS ★

seen you two in my classroom before, you *must* be Astro and Astra!"

With a nervous smile, Astro gives a gentle nod. *Oh, boy,* he thinks, knowing his sister enjoys feeding off of other people's energy. *If you're looking for energy and charm, she can give it to you.*

Astra's face lights up. "Ms. White!" she greets enthusiastically to match the teacher's energy. She reaches out and vigorously shakes Ms. White's hand. "It's a pleasure to meet you! And, may I say, this" — gesturing toward the room — "is a lovely room."

Ms. White raises her eyebrows. "O-Oh . . . well, thank you," she says, growing a bit less enthusiastic. "I'm surprised. You're quite . . . charismatic."

"Of course! When I want to be," Astra quips with a grin.

"And quick too!" she compliments, reaching out and grabbing Astra's items out of her hands.

As Ms. White reaches for Astro's notebook, he instinctively glares and tightens his grip.

Seeing Ms. White extending her arm toward Astro, Astra quickly steps between them. Changing her playful tone to a serious one, she stares into the teacher's eyes and says, "Please. Don't."

★ THE SIBLINGS' DOUBLE TROUBLES ★

"Oh, no! I just thought I'd hold on to it while you two introduce yourselves."

"That's his personal notebook," she explains without blinking. "It's extremely important to him. Please, just leave it be."

Ms. White quickly retracts her arm. "O-Oh-I, o-of course," she says, stumbling over a few words. She takes a breath and recollects herself. "I'm sorry. I didn't mean to make you nervous."

Astro breathes, relaxes his grip, and nods to accept her apology.

Ms. White smiles and nods back. Looking over at her class, she sees her students staring and whispering. She steps aside and centers herself in front of her students. Taking command of her classroom, Ms. White shouts, "One, two, three! Eyes on me!"

"One, two! Eyes on you!" the class hollers in unison before quieting down.

"Like I've been saying all week, we have two new students joining us," Ms. White says before looking at the Seeker siblings. "Okay. Why don't you two say your names and one fact about yourselves."

Astra inhales and feels her heart pound as she feels a rush of adrenaline. Using the desk arrangement to her

★ THE SEEKER SIBLINGS ★

advantage, Astra strolls into the middle and surrounds herself with everyone's eyes. Soaking up the attention, she lets out a cheeky grin. Widening her eyes as if under a spotlight, she stares up and down the rows of desks. Astra takes one more deep breath before starting her introduction.

"My name's Astra," she says as she elegantly spins in a circle. "And my interesting fact is" — stopping and staring straight ahead at the middle row of desks — "*I have violet eyes!*"

Immediately following Astra's introduction, Astro stares and furrows his eyebrows. "M-My name is Astro," he says softly. "I-I also have violet eyes."

The class erupts from their introductions, and Ms. White gathers Astro and Astra at the front of the room by the board.

She crouches down and meets them at eye level. "Okay!" she says, speaking loud enough to be heard over the noise. "In that middle row, there are two seats on opposite ends. If you two can agree, you can pick where you sit. Fair?"

Astra grins. "Fair as a carnival," she replies as Astro nods.

Ms. White chuckles and stands up.

★ THE SIBLINGS' DOUBLE TROUBLES ★

The twins walk back through the desk arrangement toward the middle row. Using the noisy atmosphere to their advantage, they briefly talk with each other.

"So?" asks Astra, glancing around and smiling at her new classmates.

"A class of twenty-two, with me and you," Astro mumbles quickly. "Lots of raised eyebrows and just as many widened eyes. There were four dropped jaws and three yawns. You?"

"I'd say ten curious, five excited, and several couldn't care," she spits out, splitting off to her left and sitting at the end of the row.

Astro breaks to the right and keeps his eyes down. He locates the empty desk, shuffles over, and sits in the seat.

As they sit at their new desks, Ms. White shouts, "Piece of pie, piece of cake!"

"We're alert! We're awake!" the class yells back simultaneously.

"Okay, it's been a bit of a crazy start," she says. "But, as usual, we *will* do our morning meeting. So, come on up!" She gestures toward herself, encouraging everyone to join her at the front of the room. "Don't worry! You'll have all year to get to know your new classmates."

★ THE SEEKER SIBLINGS ★

The Seeker siblings follow everyone to the front of the room and sit on the rug by the board.

Ms. White and her twenty-two students start their daily morning meeting routine.

— CHAPTER TWO —

The Second Siblings

With their morning meeting coming to an end, the students lift themselves up from the rug. Everyone begins walking back to their desks — including Ms. White.

As Ms. White grabs a clipboard from her desk, she instructs, "Please get your math and reading homework out so it's ready when I come around."

Astro waits in his seat and observes most of his new classmates digging inside their desks for their homework assignments. A moment later, he notices his only desk neighbor leaning in from his right.

The boy whispers, "H-Hey, I'm Jack. I hope we can become friends." Jack stops leaning and sits back in his seat. But after a few seconds, he leans over again. "I, uh, I'm sure you get this all the time. But I think your eyes are crazy cool! I've never seen anything like them!"

Astro gives a faint smile and nods. *I know I saw him with wide eyes and a dropped jaw during our introductions,* Astro thinks. *Is he one of the excited ones Astra told me about? Oh! I need to respond. But what should I say? Wait . . . why isn't he getting his math homework?*

Astro gulps and hesitantly opens his mouth. "I-If you have your homework," he whispers, "you'd better get it out."

"Oh, I *would,* but —"

"But you don't have it," Ms. White interrupts, walking behind them. "Right?"

Jack sighs. "R-Right. But I have —"

"Reading. Got it," she says, marking the sheet of paper snapped into her clipboard. "It's Friday! So next week's a new week!"

Jack nods and begins putting his homework away.

Overhearing the conversation, Astro squints and furrows his eyebrows. *No math homework? I wonder why he doesn't —*

"Oh!" Jack gasps, shutting his desk and unknowingly interrupting Astro's thoughts. "So" — dipping his head as if telling a secret — "are those contacts? Or were you born with violet eyes?"

★ THE SIBLINGS' DOUBLE TROUBLES ★

"Th-They're naturally violet," mutters Astro, still wondering about Jack's homework. "Um-Jake, can I ask why —"

"Jack," he interrupts.

"Huh? Oh! I-I'm sorry. Jack," Astro corrects with a nod. "C-Can I ask why you don't have your math homework?"

"Well, I . . . I just don't," he grumbles before changing his tone and the subject. "Oh! But that's your sister, right? Based on your introductions, you seem like the shy one."

"Er-well, cautious," Astro says, continuing to think. *Did he leave it at home? Maybe he dislikes math and never does it,* he guesses. *Just let it be! If he doesn't want to do his homework, that's his deal.*

"Yeah, okay," says Jack, partially brushing off Astro's comment. "Wait, so is your vision purple? Or do you have a purplish filter? Which shade of purple is it?"

Astro raises an eyebrow. "Jack," he replies, "what color are your eyes?"

"Hm? Me? Brown."

"Mh-hmm . . . and what colors do you see?"

★ THE SEEKER SIBLINGS ★

"Uhh, all of them?" Jack answers. "Oh, right." His cheeks burn a light red. "Ack, I'm sorry. It's just, violet eyes are so — Well, I've never — Ah! You know!"

Astro chuckles through his nose with a subtle grin. "What about you? Do you have any siblings?"

Jack hesitates, and his face tenses up. "Yeah. I do. But she's not as cool as Astra," he mutters. "Hey! How about we switch?"

"No thank you," he says without hesitating. "So, is she older? Younger?"

"Nah. She's actually over there" — jerking his head to the right toward the opposite end of the row — "talking with your sister."

Astro turns and peeks but can't get a clear view and ditches the idea. "S-So, do you and your sister not get along?" he asks, following up on his comment about switching sisters.

"I-It's complicated. Actually, please just forget I said anything."

Astro nods, and they wait for Ms. White to complete her homework check.

★ THE SIBLINGS' DOUBLE TROUBLES ★

Meanwhile, while Astro and Jack are busy with their introductions, Astra's eyes shimmer across the room.

Yay! Astra celebrates inside her head. *I get to sit by a girl who looked excited!* Watching Ms. White begin her homework check on Astro's side of the room, she looks to her left and glances at the girl sitting in the adjacent desk.

"Hey neighbor," Astra greets with a friendly smile. "My name's —"

"Wait! Let me guess! I'm thinking . . . Anna?" the girl teases, purposefully saying the wrong name.

Astra smirks, picking up on the girl's sarcasm. *"Close,"* she says before poking back. "Well, at least you got the right letter!"

The girl grins and lightheartedly shrugs with a loose head shake. "Dang. And here I thought we had matching names."

"Well, Anna?" Astra says, watching her nod. "I hope we can be friends!"

"No, *best* friends!" exclaims Anna.

"The *bestest* of friends!" Astra says louder.

"So bestest of friends, people can't *help* but write about us!"

"WE'LL BE FAMOUS!" shouts Astra.

"YEAH! WE'LL BE —"

"GIRLS! Please!" Ms. White interrupts with a stern, concerned face, standing a few students away. "Inside voices."

Astra and Anna apologize and take her face as a warning.

"Anyways, I'm Anna," she says with a half-hearted smile.

Astra smiles and thinks, *was that a real smile?* "It's nice to meet you. My name's Astra," she says, looking at Anna's desk. "I see you have your homework. Very responsible of you!"

"Yeah. But please don't say that too loud, or my obnoxious brother is going to have a fit."

"Oh? Is your brother in this class?" she asks, lifting her head and looking around the room.

"Y-Yeah," Anna says with a sigh. "He's over at the other end with your brother."

Catching a glimpse of her brother, Astra stops looking and focuses her attention back on Anna. "A-Are you two fighting?" she asks, trying not to overstep.

Anna pauses before mumbling, "I-It's complicated." She forces another smile. "It's nothing. He's just . . . being irritating. That's all."

★ THE SIBLINGS' DOUBLE TROUBLES ★

Another one? Astra thinks. "Yeah," she says with a sympathetic expression. "Siblings can be like that sometimes."

Noticing Anna's deflated spirit, Astra calms her emotions, body language, and energy to match.

Astra's mind races as she takes a few peeks at Anna. *What's up with the fake smiles? Why can't we talk about homework? And why the heck would her brother get upset? Maybe the assignments are easy for her, and she doesn't want to brag?*

Ms. White strolls behind them. "Great job, Anna! It looks good!" she praises, marking it on her clipboard and moving to the last row.

Astra sees Anna nod with another fake smile. *What the heck! Maybe she's just having a bad day,* she thinks, inventing another made-up reason and adding it to her growing list.

"What about you?" Anna asks while putting away her homework. "Do you and Astro fight?"

Astra looks at the ceiling. *I mean, we do,* she thinks. "Y-Yeah, sometimes."

"Oh! W-Well, it's good to know another pair of siblings fight."

Hm? Does she think siblings always get along with one another? That's bonkers! "W-Well, I think everyone fights every now and then," Astra says. "Oo! But you want to know something that you can't tell Astro?"

Anna glances over, and curiosity washes over her face. "Yeah, what is it?"

"Other than our parents, I think the person I trust the most would be my brother. And if I were to need him, I know he'd be there for me."

"Aw, that's sweet!" Anna confesses, letting out a quiet sigh. "You're lucky . . . I-I don't know if I could say the same about *my* brother."

Feeling Anna's heart sink even further, Astra closes her eyes and presses her lips together. *Really Astra,* she scolds. *That was SO not the right time to mention your relationship with Astro.*

"I-I'm sorry," apologizes Astra.

"No, don't be!" Anna says. "Honestly, we usually get along. But some stuff has been happening . . . and yeah."

"I'm sorry," she repeats — this time with a sympathetic expression. "I don't know either of you that well, but if there's anything I can do to help —"

"Thanks," Anna mutters. "But I don't think so."

★ THE SIBLINGS' DOUBLE TROUBLES ★

Astra nods and turns her attention to the front of the room.

Ms. White sets her clipboard on her desk and begins the class schedule for the day.

The rest of the morning, Astro mainly keeps to himself, only occasionally talking to Jack. At the same time, Astra uses her bubbly personality to befriend Anna. And they both watch Ms. White, their classmates, and the dynamics of their new classroom.

— CHAPTER THREE —

Puzzling Playground Problems

As the morning ticks by, the students can practically taste the sweet relief of recess. They all sit at the edge of their seats in anticipation.

Ms. White notices her restless students and sneaks a peek at the clock. Grinning and looking at her class, Ms. White slowly opens her mouth. Pausing, she sees several students flinch. She does her best to keep from smiling. After having fun and teasing her students, she quickly shouts, "Time for recess!"

Before she can finish her sentence, several students pop up from their seats and rush to start a line by the doorway.

Astra and Anna join their jumpy classmates and rush to join the forming line. The girls happily get spots near the middle.

☆ ☆ ☆ ☆

★ THE SIBLINGS' DOUBLE TROUBLES ★

Opposite Astra and Anna, Astro and Jack remain in their seats. After waiting for the rest of their classmates to join the line, they hop in at the end.

Standing behind Jack, Astro watches a woman in a neon-yellow vest appear in the doorway. A few seconds later, she disappears, and the line follows her out of the room.

"Move!" a student whines.

"Stop stepping on me!" cries another.

"Walk faster!" snaps a different classmate.

The recess monitor ignores the boisterous students and continues leading everyone through the hallways.

Eventually, they reach the doors and are set free. The line disperses as almost everybody sprints outside and down one of the two paths — one leading toward the playground and the other connecting to the blacktop.

Instead of running and screaming, Astro takes a deep breath of fresh air and walks down the slightly descending path toward the blacktop. He arrives last.

Astro scans the hectic area. *Hopscotch, jump rope, basketball, and foursquare,* he lists in his head. *Oh! They even have lawn games.* Instead of testing out the lawn games, Astro sees Jack at a nearby basketball hoop and joins him.

"Oh, hey!" calls Jack, holding out a squishy basketball. "Did you want a turn?"

Astro raises his eyebrows, widens his eyes, and stares at the oblong basketball. "N-No. That's okay. But thank you for asking," he declines, grinning and watching the football-shaped basketball trying its best to live up to its full potential.

Jack shoots the ball, and they watch it smack against the backboard and plop onto the blacktop. "Oh, I'm sorry! It's your first time out here. Did you want to look around?" he asks before retrieving the ball and rejoining Astro. "What do you like to do at recess?"

"I usually swing and talk with Astra."

"O-Oh, yeah?" he says, stopping mid-shot and gulping. "My sister likes swinging too. Would, uh, w-would you like to see the swings?"

"I *should* probably spend some time with —"

"Then let's go!" he says, not wanting to be the rain on Astro's parade. Jack runs to the portable ball holder, tosses the deflated basketball inside, and hurries off the blacktop toward the playground.

Astro dashes after him.

★ THE SIBLINGS' DOUBLE TROUBLES ★

They rush off the faded blacktop and up a tiny hill before hurdling the low playground border and turning right.

Arriving at the swing set near the playground, Astro and Jack look around.

"Do you see them?" asks Jack.

Astro searches up and down the long line of swings. "Ah . . . surprisingly, no," he answers, noticing the field beyond the swings. "That's a big field."

"Yeah! As you can see, they usually play two-hand touch football during recess."

Astro squints and furrows his eyebrows. "Ah, right. So, you have a ginormous field for recess football?"

Jack grins. "No, no, no, no. The school also uses it for special events. Like track and field day. History day. Oh! Sometimes the school carnivals use it. Uh . . . graduation *might* be out there, but I'm not sure."

Astro nods and focuses back on the swings. "Hmph. I thought Astra would be swinging. But it looks like I'm wrong," he admits.

"Not so fast!" Jack says with a grin. "There's another area we haven't checked."

Astro raises an eyebrow and looks over. "Yeah?"

"Follow me!" Jack runs off behind the playground.

★ THE SEEKER SIBLINGS ★

Astro races after him.

☆ ☆ ☆ ☆

In contrast, after passing through the doors, Astra and Anna scream, jump, and sprint on the path leading toward the playground.

Halfway to the park, the asphalt pathway is replaced with a mix of dirt and grass.

The girls bolt up the small hill. Astra jumps and balances on the playground border. Inhaling through her nose, she smells the earthly outside air.

Exhaling, Astra lets out a satisfied groan of approval. "Smells like playground," she jokes to amuse herself.

Stepping inside the playground border, Astra lands on the layer of brown woodchips. She wiggles her toes inside her shoes and feels the slightly uneven ground through the soles.

"So? How is it?" Anna asks after letting Astra soak up her surroundings.

"It's nice," she says. "The playground's huge! But it looks kind of . . . old."

Anna chuckles. "You got *that* right!"

★ THE SIBLINGS' DOUBLE TROUBLES ★

"Oo! Swings!" Astra squeals, running to the right side of the border. She stops as she approaches the swing set. "You guys have more swings than our old school."

"Oh, yeah?" Anna says, running up behind her. "I, uh, I should tell you . . ." Anna closes her eyes.

"What?"

Shaking her head, Anna says, "You can't jump off of the swings to try and clear the border and land on the field."

"Uh, okay?" Astra squints. "Wait, but why is that a rule?"

Anna stops herself from laughing, letting out a small snort. "Yeah. *Why* indeed!"

"Oof," she grunts, shaking her head and imagining the worst-case scenario.

They stare at the swing set stretching across the entire right-side border.

"Y'know, there's some more in another area if you want to see," suggests Anna.

Astra grins, and they run around the playground. Hopping over the border, they jog across a small patch of grass and approach a separate area.

"So?" asks Anna. "What do you think?"

★ THE SEEKER SIBLINGS ★

Astra stares at the enormous chain of swings in the center of the boxed-in space.

"It's ... beautiful," she remarks, stepping over the border and onto the multicolored pebbles. She runs to a pair of empty swings. "First!" Astra teases, sitting down.

"S-Second?" says Anna, playing along and grabbing the swing beside Astra. "I'm so happy you like swinging! Now I'll have a partner!"

"Oh? Your brother doesn't swing with you?"

"Psh, *no*," she grunts before making a sad expression. "Er-well, I mean ... sometimes. But not recently! Does Astro swing with you?"

"Yeah! Like every day! You could probably tell, but he likes to keep to himself."

"It did seem like you were more outgoing."

Astra nods. "Yeah. Honestly, I'm surprised he hasn't found his way over —"

"Wait!" Anna interrupts. "Is that him?"

Focusing her violet eyes near the playground, Astra sees Astro and Jack walking toward them.

Despite the chaotic students running around, Astra feels the increasing tension as Astro and Jack approach.

The two pairs of twins are face-to-face for the first time since meeting.

★ THE SIBLINGS' DOUBLE TROUBLES ★

Not realizing the critical moment, Astro says, "I see you have a classmate showing you around."

Astra's eyes widen, nearly popping out of her head as her thoughts race. *Oh my gosh! I mean, he's not wrong. But did he have to say it like that?*

Astra playfully giggles, trying to play off Astro's ill-timed remark. "What! Anna isn't *just* a classmate!" she says, trying to lighten the mood and give Astro a hint. "She's my new best friend!"

Astro doesn't get it and shifts his eyes toward Jack. "Oh. Wait, are you Jack's sister?"

"Hmph, more like Jack's *my* brother," she snaps, not wanting to be Jack's anything.

Astro gulps. "Er-I-I didn't mean it like that," he says. "I-I'm sorry if I misspoke."

"Quit being mean to my friend!" Jack barks.

Anna ignores him.

Astra gulps, hearing and sensing everyone's apprehensiveness. *Oh no! What do I do? What should I do? What can I do? I could . . . try helping them get along? I guess I can try,* she decides. Astra begins chuckling and redirects everyone's attention to herself.

She sneaks a subtle breath, and her giggles turn into tiny whimpers. "Y-You two seem so nice," Astra praises.

"But" — squeezing out a couple of tears — "seeing you two argue like this makes me so sad!"

Astro watches Astra attempt to tilt the conversation in her favor. *Wow. Tears and all,* he thinks.

"Well, if she would stop stealing my homework, we wouldn't have a problem!" attacks Jack.

Astro's attention shifts, and he furrows his eyebrows. *Hm? Stolen homework?* He squints. *Is this connected to this morning?*

"I've told you a hundred times! I haven't touched your homework!" Anna snaps. "*I* do my *own* homework. So why don't you return my necklace!"

Keeping her head down, Astra wipes her fake tears and overhears Anna's comment. *Return necklace? Is this what they've been fighting about? Is this the reason she keeps flashing those half-hearted smiles?*

"Oh please!" shouts Jack. "Like *you* know how to do homework!"

"Tsh! Apparently better than you since *I* have it in class!"

"Oh, real nice. *Reeaal nice.* Why would I even *want* your necklace? That doesn't make any sense!"

"Because you think I take your homework!" she yells.

★ THE SIBLINGS' DOUBLE TROUBLES ★

"Think?" Jack retorts, rolling his eyes. *"I know!"*

Astro freezes from the yelling and shouting.

As they continue, Astra's thoughts race. *Oh, no. This is bad. We're just going back and forth and not getting anywhere. Should I use humor to try to lighten the mood? Yeah, I can try. Go! Go!*

"Looks like we have some mysteries on our hands!" Astra jokes, lifting both hands and pretending to look through two magnifying glasses. "And who doesn't love myster —"

"There's no mystery since I already know *she* took it," Jack repeats.

"Believe whatever you want! But you shouldn't have taken my favorite necklace!"

"*Boo-hoo.* At least people don't think you're a lazy slacker who doesn't do their homework!"

Oh no, oh no, oh no, oh no, Astra repeats in her head. *What am I supposed to do now?* Looking up, she notices Astro's frozen expression.

"Okay!" cries Astra, feeling the conversation tiptoeing toward dangerous territories. "Why don't we all just take some deep breaths. I'm sure —"

"Ms. White's class!" a recess monitor calls using a red-and-white megaphone. "Time to line up for lunch!"

Hearing the call, Astro thaws out.

Astro and Astra silently exhale and stare at each other with wide eyes. Simultaneously, they think the same thing: *We got saved from that one.*

As the recess monitor repeats herself several more times, they run to the blacktop. Joining their classmates, they line up at the corner connected to the asphalt path. Moments later, a recess monitor leads everyone up the pathway and into the building.

Navigating the halls and passing their classroom, the class reaches the serving area connected to the cafeteria.

— CHAPTER FOUR —

Discussions

Entering the cafeteria with their trays, they're engulfed by a roar of chatter — a combination of their classmates and students in several other classes.

Scanning the gym-sized lunchroom, Astro and Astra see several big posters hanging on the walls. Some have motivational messages and inspirational photos, whereas others have school-related memes.

Glancing up, the twins watch a couple lights flicker. They relax their necks and look ahead. They notice the cafeteria is packed with two columns of long chocolate-brown tables — creating an aisle through the middle.

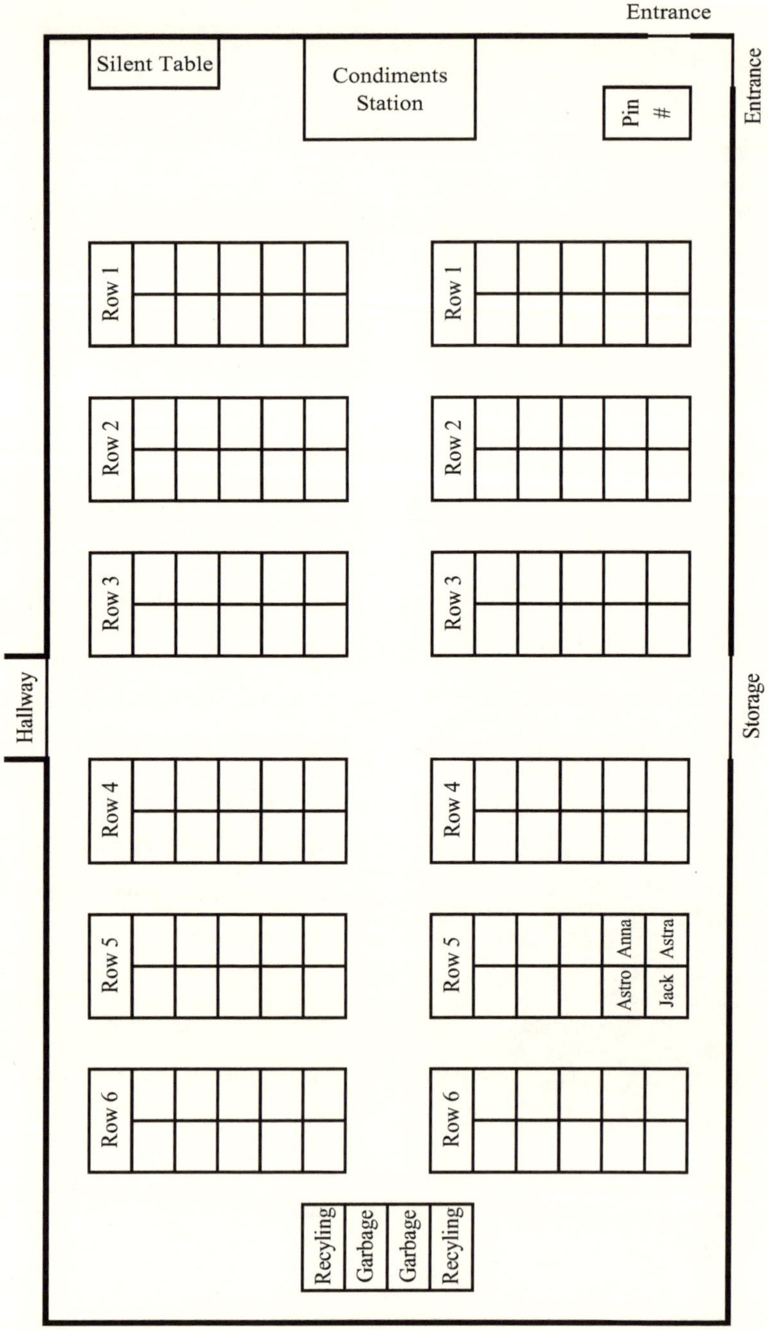

Entrance
Silent Table
Condiments Station
Pin #
Entrance
Row 1
Row 1
Row 2
Row 2
Row 3
Row 3
Hallway
Storage
Row 4
Row 4
Row 5
Row 5
Anna
Astra
Astro
Jack
Row 6
Row 6
Recyling
Garbage
Garbage
Recyling

★ THE SIBLINGS' DOUBLE TROUBLES ★

"Hey!" Jack calls, walking past them with his tray of food. "Follow me!"

Letting Jack take the lead, the Seeker siblings stroll down the middle aisle. Astro and Astra feel like two fish out of water. Reaching the fifth row of tables, they turn left and head to the opposite end — near the wall.

The boys sit down — Jack on the end — and share part of the bench, with their backs facing the sixth row of tables. The girls sit on the bench across from them — kitty-corner from their siblings.

Astro turns toward Jack and asks, "Do they really let you sit anywhere?"

Jack snorts as he cuts off a chuckle. "No way. Not a chance! Each class gets a row of tables. We have this one and" — tilting his head toward the fifth table across the aisle — "that one. So you *can* pick where you sit, as long as it's at one of these two tables."

Astro nods. "Ah, that makes more sense," he admits, taking a bite of his lunch.

For several minutes, the four of them sit and stare at each other — only opening their mouths to take a bite of food. Instead of chattering and conversing like everyone else in the lunchroom, the end of their table is silent — creating a looming awkwardness.

★ THE SEEKER SIBLINGS ★

So uncomfortable, thinks Astra. *Should I try to say something to ease the tension? It didn't work too well earlier. But I guess I can try agai —*

"I'm sorry," Anna apologizes, swallowing a mouthful of food. "It probably sucks hearing us whine about our problems." She sighs. "Truthfully, I'm surprised at how well you two get along."

"Yeah, I'm jealous!" Jack agrees with his sister — for the first time since getting them together. "What's your secret? Oh! It's because you two have similar names, isn't it?"

Astro and Astra smile at each other.

"We're *told* they both mean star or something similar," says Astro.

"Yeah!" Astra exclaims. "Our parents had some other names picked out. But when we were born, they took one look at our eyes and changed them."

Astro nods and adds, "Our dad named Astra, and our mom named me."

"Oooo! That's so cuute!" squeals Anna.

"I know it!" Astra gushes. "They said our eyes reminded them of space. And that we should always reach for the stars!"

★ THE SIBLINGS' DOUBLE TROUBLES ★

Astro's smile vanishes, and a worried expression appears. "Mh-hmm. B-But I'm not sure I want to be an astronaut. Maybe I could work behind the scenes of one instead."

Astra squints and scrunches her nose. "Astro, I don't think they meant it in a literal way. More of a —" She sighs. "Er-never mind."

Jack and Anna let out a small chuckle.

"I mean, not only that," says Jack, "but even your black-and-white hair is sort of space-like! Or is it dyed?"

Astra smiles. "Well, *that* was just a coincidence since they didn't know it would be like this until later. But yeah," — combing through her bright white hair strands near her right ear — "I have this small group." She stops and gestures to Astro. "But if you look closely, Astro has white strands scattered into his black ones."

Seeing Jack and Anna squinting and staring at his hair, Astro tilts his head toward his chest. As he moves, the scattered white hair strands catch the light and appear to twinkle, copying the stars on a clear night in the jet-black sky.

"Oooh!" Jack and Anna coo at the same time.

Astra giggles. "Our parents warned us that our hair may turn white sooner rather than later."

★ THE SEEKER SIBLINGS ★

"Not your hair, bestie!" cries Anna.

"My hair!" she emphasizes, playfully sobbing. "I'm too young to be a grandma!"

Jack swallows a bite of food. "Seeing how you already have some, I guess I wouldn't be all that shocked either. But you two could probably pull off white."

"Yeah, it'll probably be white before most people's," Astro admits. "But I wonder if it'll stay white or turn gray."

"Even if it does," says Jack, "if your hair is white by then, it'd be almost impossible to tell the difference. Y'know?"

Astro nods. "Yeah, you're probably right."

"Don't worry!" says Anna, continuing to play along with Astra. "White has to be the easiest to dye! That's what makes it so easy for old people!"

Astra's fake sobs turn into cracks of laughter.

Anna gasps. "Oops! I'm sorry. I didn't mean for that to sound —"

"No, no! It was funny!" reassures Astra.

Anna gives an embarrassed grin.

Astra gasps and lightly smacks the tabletop. "Wait! Astro! We could dye our hair and be matching!"

★ THE SIBLINGS' DOUBLE TROUBLES ★

Astro scrunches his nose and flashes an unconvincing smile.

Astra giggles.

Watching the Seeker siblings interact, Jack squints. "You two must spend a lot of time together, huh? I-It's just . . . you seem so comfortable with one another."

"Yeah!" says Astra. "Before moving, we spent a lot of time together solving mys —"

Cough! Cough! Cough! Astro coughs violently into a closed fist while shooting piercing daggers into Astra's violet eyes.

Astra flashes Astro a look of her own — not that he understands — before clearing her throat. "Er . . . w-we solved, uh . . ." — closing her eyes — "m-m-mis . . . cellaneous sudoku puzzles and word finds," she improvises.

"Mh-hmm," Astro hums quickly. "People say we make quite a team."

"Yeah," agrees Jack. "It does seem like you're better together than apart."

Astro squints and dips one of his eyebrows, confused by his friend's remark. "Well, *yeah*. We *are* family," he says, taking a bite of his lunch — not seeing Jack and Anna lock eyes for half a second.

★ THE SEEKER SIBLINGS ★

Immediately after finishing their lunches, the group splits back into pairs — Astro with Jack and Astra with Anna — for the rest of the school day.

Stepping off the bus, Astro and Astra walk to their house.

The Seeker household isn't anything fancy, but Astro and Astra find it comfy anyway. Feeling more comfortable within the walls of their home, the twins relax and walk into the living room.

Astro sits on one couch while Astra sits on another. They start a movie — one they've seen a million times — and begin their homework. But only making it past a few previews, Astra rests her head on the back of the couch and looks at Astro.

"So, what do you think?" Astra asks in a calm, serene tone — unlike her usual public appearance.

"What do I think . . . about what?" asks Astro in a similar tone.

"Are we going to help them?"

Astro gulps and stares at the television. "Help . . . *who?* You'll have to be more specific."

"Don't play dumb!" she snaps. "I know you have a difficult time reading between the lines, but I know you know this one!"

★ THE SIBLINGS' DOUBLE TROUBLES ★

Furrowing his eyebrows, he exhales quietly. Glancing over, Astro sees Astra blinking excessively with a wide smile.

Astro turns and looks back at the television. "Nope," he answers. Astro doesn't hear anything and peeks back at Astra, only to see her pouting. "Astra, no! It's not our responsibility."

"Please?"

"No!"

"Please, please?" Astra pleads.

"What? No! Why *should* we? Do you want to move again?"

"Hey, it's not *our* fault people asked for help. We're just good at helping. Is that a crime? Huh? And why couldn't we tell Jack and Anna that we used to solve myster —"

"We don't need the attention," he spits out. "And, technically, it's *exactly* our fault —"

"But it's not our fault people have *problems.*"

Astro grumbles, "Did you *want* to move to another town? City? Place?"

"N-No, not really."

"Do you *want* more trouble for ourselves? *And* our parents?"

★ THE SEEKER SIBLINGS ★

"N-No."

"Do you want a different house?"

"No!"

"A different school?"

"NO! But Mom and Dad always tell us to help if we can! So it's our responsibility to —"

"No! It's not! It's theirs!" shouts Astro.

Astra mumbles under her breath, upset with Astro's argument. "What do you think Mom and Dad would say if they knew we stood by when we could've helped?"

"I'm not them, so *I* wouldn't know —"

"WRONG! You're one of the only people that *would* know besides themselves."

Astro grumbles again before muttering, "Sometimes you're really irritating."

Taking a deep breath and closing his eyes, his violet eyes begin darting side to side beneath his eyelids. Astro begins creating a vivid scenario inside his mind.

He inserts all the facts, adds an environment, and remembers the habits of their parents — their past conversations, stories, experiences, and more.

"Mom, Dad," he says inside the vision while mumbling it in real life. "If there's a mystery at school, would you want us to help?"

★ THE SIBLINGS' DOUBLE TROUBLES ★

Astro watches them think inside his vision.

Eventually, Mrs. Seeker opens her mouth. "If you can do it without putting yourself in danger, I think helping is a great idea. As you know, helping others can fill your heart. But remember our discussion about being careful and laying low," she says with a warm smile.

"If you can help someone in need," Mr. Seeker adds, "I think you should do what you can."

Astro opens his eyes and snaps back to reality. Looking over, he sees Astra eagerly waiting for his answer.

"Mom reminded me about being careful and laying low," he says before letting out a deep sigh. "But... they *would* want us to help."

"Yay!" she cheers.

Astro furrows his eyebrows and uses his last idea. "But who's to say there's anything *to* help?"

"Huh? What do you mean?"

Astro lightly closes his eyelids and raises one of his eyebrows. "It *could* be that Jack's not doing his homework. Then, maybe he stole Anna's necklace and won't confess," he explains.

"But —"

"Or *maybe* they're *both* to blame," he adds. "Maybe Anna *is* stealing his homework. That would mean there

★ THE SEEKER SIBLINGS ★

isn't *actually* anything to solve. It's just a case of fighting siblings." He smiles smugly as if he's solved the mystery.

Astra squints and furrows her eyebrows. "But Anna didn't seem interested in Jack's homework," she says before her eyes light up. "Did *Jack* give you the impression he's a thief who steals important and personal items?"

Astro's smug face fades. "Oh. W-Well, no. But..." He sharply exhales. "Fine! We'll try. But I can't promise we'll solve them, okay? And we're only helping if they promise not to tell anyone about anything. Okay?"

"Yes, sir!" she says with a playful salute. She looks up to her left and squints. "Y-Yes, sir?"

"You said that twice."

"Well, you asked two questions."

"I... I suppose I did," Astro says, chewing his inner lip and thinking about their decision.

Minutes later, Astro's head begins pounding. Astro hears his heartbeat pumping inside his ears as a splitting migraine takes hold of him.

"Astra, will you — Ah!" he cries, holding his head and covering his eyes.

Astra springs up from the couch. "On it!" she calls, running to the nearby bathroom.

★ THE SIBLINGS' DOUBLE TROUBLES ★

She returns to Astro — who is lying down on the couch — and hands him his medicine.

Taking his prescribed medication, Astro takes it easy until it starts working. Eventually, they work through their homework and wait for their parents to arrive home. They relax for the rest of the night as a family.

Completing their nightly routines, Astro and Astra retire to their rooms. They fall asleep and start their weekend.

☆ ☆ ☆ ☆

Elsewhere in town, Jack and Anna step off their bus. Walking to their house, they keep several meters of space between them. As they step through the doorway, they manage to get a few feet closer to each other. But after removing their shoes, they dart to their rooms and keep to themselves.

Even as their parents arrive home, Jack and Anna stay in their rooms.

For Jack and Anna's parents, getting their children together — much less in a pleasant mood toward one another — is trickier than corralling an entire classroom of squirrely children.

★ THE SEEKER SIBLINGS ★

During dinner, Jack, Anna, and their parents spend most of their time sitting silently. After finishing, Jack and Anna return to their bedrooms.

Over the weekend, they spend the majority of their time in their rooms or with their parents. But rarely together as a family.

— CHAPTER FIVE —

Astro's Investigation

On Monday, the Seeker siblings use the same route to reach Ms. White's classroom. Arriving before most of their classmates, they talk by Astra's desk.

Several minutes later, Jack and Anna enter the room with a few other students.

Astra takes a slow, deep breath as Jack and Anna approach. "Before you say anything," Astra starts, taking control of the conversation, "Astro and I talked over the weekend, and we've decided to try and help you two."

"Ohh, *sweet*," says Jack, nodding like a loose bobble-head. "Help us with . . . what?"

Astra squints as her head twitches to the left. "Uh, w-with all the troubles?" Her eyes pop back open. "Like, we're going to try and figure out who's stealing your homework." Astra turns to Anna. "And the person who stole your necklace."

Hearing this, Jack and Anna exchange glares and play a game of chicken — with neither of them backing down.

"That's correct," confirms Astro, oblivious to their showdown. "But you'll have to promise to keep our help a secret. Anything you see. Anything you hear. Anything you *think* you might know. Whatever it may be. Actually, don't even tell people that we were involved, okay?"

Listening to Astro, their glares morph into expressions of curiosity and confusion. They turn to Astro, nod, and agree.

Astra grins, rubbing and twisting her palms together. "Oh-ho-ho! This is gonna be *sweet!* The stars align for anoth — uh, a-a f-for a mystery!" she says, saving herself from accidentally spilling their secret.

"Aw! Bestie!" squeals Anna. "That's so cute! Because both of your names mean star?"

Astra giggles. "Yeah."

Jack shifts his weight to one leg and squints at Astro. "Then whose are you solving first?" he asks with a suspicious and combative tone.

★ THE SIBLINGS' DOUBLE TROUBLES ★

Astro narrows his eyes and sharply exhales. "Both! And" — grabbing his special notebook and an ordinary pencil — "we'll start right now."

Opening his notebook and titling the pages — two for each of them — he keeps the mysteries separate. He turns to Anna and says, "Alright, please . . . be as honest as possible. Have you ever taken Jack's homework?"

"No! Of course not!" she spits out defensively, nearly cutting him off. "A-And, well" — reaching up and itching her eyebrow — "even if I had, I would've put it back. So it's not *me* stealing his homework."

Astro squints and writes in his notebook.

Astra sees her friend squirm in place as her cheeks turn a subtle rose pink. She notices a few sweat beads gathering on her forehead and feels the shift in pressure.

Hoping to protect the peace, Astra steps in and asks, "How about you, Jack? Have you ever taken Anna's necklace?"

"Well, I mean. I've *thought* about it. But I wouldn't actually —"

"THERE! YOU SEE!" yells Anna, jumping down her brother's throat.

"Woah, woah, woah," says Astro, continuing to write. "Breathe. There's no reason to get upset —"

"BUT HE JUST ADMITTED TO IT!"

Astro stops writing and lifts his eyes out of his notebook. "No, actions and thoughts are different," he tries explaining.

"WHAT! COME ON! IT'S BASICALLY THE SAME THI —"

"No, it's not, Anna. Please! Try and breathe," Astro interjects before revealing, "*You* actually said something similar. Because if you *'had'* taken your brother's homework, you'd *return* it. Which means you *have* taken it before, correct?"

Anna gulps, shifts her weight to her heels, and looks away. "W-Well. N-Y, I uh . . ." she stammers, tripping over her words and thoughts before growing quiet.

"Wait!" Jack exclaims. "Does that mean —"

"STOP! No! We're not doing this!" Astro scolds. "If you say you didn't steal her necklace, we're believing you! And if Anna says she's not stealing your homework, we're believing her! Yes?"

Jack and Anna keep their mouths shut, afraid of making themselves look more guilty.

Seeing them grow silent, Astra widens her eyes and stares at the ground. *AHH!* she screams in her head. *I need to lighten the mood! How can I calm them down?*

★ THE SIBLINGS' DOUBLE TROUBLES ★

A joke? Glancing up, Astra sees Jack and Anna's tense faces. *Mm-no. Now probably isn't the right time. Maybe I should try a compliment? Yeah, that might work.*

"But either way!" says Astra, grabbing their attention. "I think both of you are WAY too nice to do these things!"

Astro continues writing, and after a few seconds, he says, "Yes. I agree."

Jack and Anna look at each other with doubtful expressions but settle down.

Phew! Thank goodness, Astra thinks as she silently exhales. *Looks like they're calming down. And, for now, they've stopped accusing each other.*

"Okay! You know what time it is!" calls Ms. White.

"Let's split up during recess," suggests Astro. "Astra and Anna. Me and Jack."

Everyone nods, and the boys scurry to their seats to start the school day.

During recess, they all follow Astro's suggestion and split up accordingly.

The boys saunter to the end of the swing set closest to the blacktop.

Sitting on the end swing, Astro places his notebook on his lap. "Can I ask you a few questions?" he asks, twisting in his seat and opening his notebook.

Barely swinging, Jack hesitantly nods, still feeling cautious from this morning.

"Alright," says Astro, not wasting any time. "Do you complete your homework every night?"

"I-I try to, yeah."

"What do you do with it afterward?"

Jack looks up and thinks before answering, "I put it in my folder. Then —"

"Your school folder?" Astro interrupts, writing inside his notebook.

Jack nods. "Then I put *that* in my backpack."

"And when do you put it away?"

"Oh! Um, usually at night since we leave early the next morning."

"Early? How early?" Astro questions.

"Ah, I mean, early enough to drop us off at the before-school program."

Astro raises an eyebrow. "Hmph! I didn't know the school had one of those," he says before continuing his questioning — some might say interrogation. "What do you do there?"

★ THE SIBLINGS' DOUBLE TROUBLES ★

"Er-mostly play games. Oh! And eat breakfast. But then I come to class, the teacher asks for it, and . . . you know the rest," Jack explains, hoping to pause Astro's stream of questions.

Astro squints. *Interesting,* he thinks, writing in his notebook. "Mm, are you good at homework?"

"I-I don't know? I think I'm okay at it," he says, shrugging his shoulders.

"I'm sorry," Astro apologizes. "I'm *actually* wondering if anyone asks to copy your homework."

Jack half-heartedly chuckles. "Yeah, no."

Astro grins. "Right, okay." He sets his pencil down inside his notebook. "Jack, are you being bullied?"

Jack hesitates and looks off to the side. "N-Nah. I mean, other than the person taking my homework!" He chuckles. "Jeez! What do they even do with it?"

Astro grins at his joke and picks up his pencil again. "So last Friday — well, and today — I noticed you still had your reading log packet." He squints. "Has that ever gone missing?"

Jack furrows his eyebrows and widens his eyes. "Huh," he grunts. "No! No, it's just my math worksheets! What does that even mean?"

★ THE SEEKER SIBLINGS ★

"I don't know," he admits, placing his pencil back down. "So, Jack! What do you like to do for fun?"

"Huh? Wait, but what does that have to do with the mystery?"

"N-Nothing," Astro admits shyly. "B-But, I also want to get to know you."

Jack gasps. "Oh! I didn't mean to — I-I'm sorry. You just caught me off guard," he explains with an embarrassed expression. "Er-I play video games, watch movies, and play outside. A-Anna used to hang out with me too. B-But not recently . . . for obvious reasons."

"Yeah, I met her a little last week. But I don't really know her. What's she like?"

Jack furrows his eyebrows and clenches his jaw. But instead of spitting out his angry thoughts, he pauses and takes a deep breath.

Eventually, Jack calmly says, "S-She's okay, I guess. As you saw, she's really upset about her necklace. But I swear, I didn't take it!" He lets out a frustrated huff. "But I wish the person who *did* take it would just give it back already."

"Yeah, me too," Astro agrees, picking up his pencil.

After writing, he stares at his notes with a spaced-out expression. Astro continues this writing and staring process for the remainder of recess.

— CHAPTER SIX —

Astra's Investigation

At the same time as Astro and Jack walk to one end of the swing set, Astra and Anna stroll to the opposite.

Watching Anna sit at the end, Astra sits on the swing beside her. *Okay, keep the conversation light,* she thinks. *I need to get information without being too serious.*

Taking a slow, deep breath, Astra widens her eyes. Cranking her charm and charisma levels to the max, Astra concentrates. Focusing on her surroundings, she starts a recording inside her mind.

Astra feels the sun shining on her skin, the gentle breeze in her hair, and the cold swing chains in her hands. She hears the students screaming and shouting, the basketballs bouncing in the distance, and the swings creaking back and forth. Astra takes in the fresh outside air and looks left at Anna.

★ THE SIBLINGS' DOUBLE TROUBLES ★

"Bestie!" Astra says with wide violet eyes. "Can you tell me more about your necklace?"

"Of course!" Anna says, smiling and responding to Astra's charm. "It's *super* small and *super* cute!"

Astra giggles. "*Super-duper!* W-What color was it?"

"Oh! Oopsies. So it was gold-colored. And it has" — glancing up — "... had? No, has my name on it. It's, like, written out all fancy-like!"

"Oo! That's so elegant!" Astra responds. "It sounds like it meant a lot to you."

"Yeah, my parents gave it to me for my last birthday, so it's . . ." She sighs. "It's important to me."

"Aw, cute! That's so sweet!"

"Gah," cries Anna, shaking her head. "I can't believe it's gone. I mean, I rarely ever took it off!"

"I-I'm sorry, bestie," she consoles. "I'm sure you've already checked your house, huh?"

"Yeah! Like a million times."

"Wow! A *gazillion* times!" she teases with a wink.

Anna giggles.

"Hmm . . ." Astra hums with an exaggerated thinking face to buy herself some time. *Ah, shoot! What should I ask now? What would Astro want to know?*

★ THE SEEKER SIBLINGS ★

Think. Think. Think. "Oh! How long has it been missing?"

Reaching up and touching her neck, Anna squeezes her lips together and slowly blows out before revealing, "M-Maybe . . . a couple of weeks?" She grimaces.

Astra flinches. "S-So for almost a month?"

"Y-Yeah," she says with a heavy heart and an even heavier sigh. "I realize it's going to be harder to find since it's been missing for so long."

"True," Astra admits before pumping her fist. "But we're going to do everything we can!"

Letting out another unconvincing smile, Anna says, "Thank you for trying to help, Astra."

Astra grins and nods as her eyelids grow heavy. Feeling her adrenaline subside, her concentration wanes, and her recording ends. Her charm and charisma levels return to normal.

Holding a wink, Astra lets out a quiet yawn and says, "I'm sorry we can't do more."

"What!" Anna cries. "Don't be silly! You're doing plenty!"

Astra nods. "So, putting the mystery aside, what do you like to do in your free time? Like after school."

★ THE SIBLINGS' DOUBLE TROUBLES ★

"I'm boring! I stay at home most of the time. I watch movies, play games, and hang out with friends. Oh! I . . . I also enjoy doing puzzles."

"What! If that's boring, sign me up for the boring club," she says before sticking out her tongue.

Anna's posture pops up in her swing. "Wait! Do you like that stuff too?"

"I think most people like doing those things," Astra comments. "And there's nothing like seeing the progress of completing puzzles."

"Yeah! There's nothing better than putting in the last piece!" Anna agrees. "Oh! I also spend time with my family. But other than that, I just hang out in my room."

"Ah, so comfy. That's actually pretty similar to *our* nights after school," Astra admits before looking away with a glassy expression.

Anna glances over and asks, "What's wrong?"

"Oh. Er-nothing. I'm just . . . thinking. Uh, you had your homework the other day."

"Y-Yeah?"

"So you must be a hard worker."

"Of course, bestie!" Anna says, with a dumbfounded expression. "Heck, if you're not trying your hardest, is it even worth it?"

★ THE SEEKER SIBLINGS ★

Astra raises her eyebrows and grins. "Y-Yeah, I suppose not," she agrees. "So, is Jack a hard worker too?"

Hearing her brother's name, Anna clenches her jaw and furrows her eyebrows. But after a few seconds, she relaxes and says, "Y-You mean with his homework? I-I mean . . ." She sighs. "You can't tell him I said this, but y-yeah. At least, *I* think so. But if you ask others, they'd probably say differently."

Astra looks straight into Anna's eyes. "Then it's a good thing I'm asking *you* and not them," she says with a cheeky grin. "After all, you're probably the only person who *really* knows him, right?"

Anna's eyes widen, and she stammers, trying to find a reply. But after flailing and searching for her words, she stops and stares at the tiny pebbles beneath her.

Switching the topic, Anna says, "Uh, any ideas about who stole the necklace?" She lifts her head and gives a hopeful smile.

"N-No, not specifically. I-I'm sorry. I'm not great at this part," admits Astra. "Usually, Astro comes up with the questions, and I ask them."

Anna squints and pauses for a second before waving her hands back and forth. "No! No! No! I think you're

★ THE SIBLINGS' DOUBLE TROUBLES ★

doing great! I swear!" she reassures. "But if that's the case, why aren't we all together?"

Astra slowly sucks air between her teeth to create a quiet hissing sound. "W-Well, Astro's better with one-on-one conversations. You might've noticed, but he gets a little nervous. So it's easier — heck and better — for everyone if we let him do one case at a time."

Anna nods upon hearing Astra's explanation. "Makes sense to me!" She sneakily squints at Astra again.

"Ms. White's Class!" calls the recess monitor with her megaphone. "Time to line up for lunch!"

They hop off their swings and walk to the blacktop with their classmates. As usual, a recess monitor leads them to the cafeteria. Astro, Astra, Jack, and Anna sit in the same seats as last week.

Anna swallows a bite of food and clears her throat. "Can I ask you two a question?"

"Of course, bestie! You can ask me anything!" Astra says as Astro nods from across the table.

Anna leans in and whispers, "S-So, last week, you told us that you two are so close because you solve miscellaneous puzzles together." She lowers her voice and whispers even softer, at a volume barely audible with all the lunchroom chatter. "B-But you were going to say mysteries, weren't you?"

The Seeker twins freeze as if turning to stone. They stare into each other's violet eyes.

Astra barely moves first, only twitching her right eyebrow upward. *Should we tell them?*

Knowing there's only one thing Astra can be asking, Astro faintly jerks his head to the left. *No.*

She squeezes her eyebrows together and lets them go. *Why not?*

Narrowing his eyes and furrowing his eyebrows, Astro holds an intense look. *No!*

Astra returns an intense gaze of her own, and they maintain their expressions for several seconds.

Eventually, Astra lets out a sigh and turns her head toward Anna. "Ah, we're just . . . curious. That's all."

Anna nods along with a tiny smirk. *"Mh-hmm,"* she hums, unconvinced, as she takes another bite of food.

They finish lunch, and the rest of the school day flies by in a flash.

After school, Astro and Astra quickly complete their homework assignments. Pausing the movie, they shift their focus to the mysteries.

★ THE SIBLINGS' DOUBLE TROUBLES ★

Astro grabs his notebook, flips to Anna's page, and shakes out his hand. "Okay!" he says, picking up a pencil and moving to the edge of the couch. "Ready!"

Astra smirks and teases, "Ready for what?"

With shiny eyes, Astro stumbles over several words before saying, "Y-You know, the recall!"

Astra holds a wink. "Hm . . . I *suppose* I can," she says, continuing to tease Astro. She sits up and gets into a comfortable position on the couch.

Astro tightens his grip and lets the lead hover a few millimeters above the page.

Astra closes her eyes and takes several slow, deep breaths. Concentrating, she clears her mind from all distractions. Pushing play on her recording, she begins her recall and returns to the playground.

Even though Astra sits at home on the couch, she begins feeling the sun's warmth on her skin. She feels the gentle breeze on her face. Astra wiggles her fingers on both hands before forming loose fists. She feels the cold, rugged structure of the swing chains in her hands. Listening to her surroundings, she hears the basketballs smacking against the asphalt in the distance. Concentrating harder, she hears students screaming and playing by the playground. Astra's ears twitch as she uses all her

★ THE SEEKER SIBLINGS ★

energy to focus even more. She hears tiny pebbles click against each other as students dash across them. As the swings pendulate, she hears them creak and squeal. Taking a deep breath, Astra feels the crisp outside air filling her lungs. She looks left — in reality and her memory — and remembers Anna in the swing beside her.

Astra begins reliving the conversation from earlier, softly mumbling Anna's answers out loud.

"It's *super* small and *super* cute!" Astra says.

Astro quickly begins writing her replies in his notebook with a big goofy grin spread across his face.

"It was gold-colored," she continues. "And it has my name on it, written out all fancy-like. For my last birthday . . . so —"

"L —" Astro interrupts before shooting his hand up and covering his mouth. With his eyes nearly popping out of his head, he stops writing.

Hearing the "L" sound, Astra's recording of her memory starts breaking and cracking, like a poor television connection. She furrows her eyebrows.

"L . . . L . . . L . . ." Astra repeats, copying the "L" sound she heard.

Astro watches his sister copy and get stuck on the sound. All he can do is watch, knowing that making an-

70

other sound — whether to explain or apologize — will only make it worse.

"L . . ." she continues, searching her recording for a similar sound. "L . . . L . . . Like a million times?" she says, continuing at another spot in the recording.

Still covering his mouth, Astro starts writing again.

"Missing a couple of weeks," Astra mumbles.

As her recording comes to an end, it freezes. With nothing more to relive, Astra opens her eyes and looks at Astro.

Astro lowers his hand from his mouth. "I-I'm sorry! I-I forgot! I swear! I'm sorry!" he apologizes repeatedly.

Astra smiles and shakes her head. "It's okay! There's no need," she says, letting out a long yawn before helping clarify several pieces of information.

After a few minutes, Astro suggests, "Maybe we can switch partners tomorrow so I can ask Anna a few questions. And you can see if anything stands out with Jack."

"Right!" Astra says, giving him a thumbs up with her left hand. She playfully pouts and switches her thumbs up to her right hand. "Right!" Astra repeats, wiggling her right hand. Seeing Astro smirk, she drops her hand into her lap. "Anyways, did anything stand out to you?"

"I mean, no. Not to *me.* But, I'm not that great with all that stuff."

"So what's the deal with his homework?" she asks, laying on her side, fighting to keep her head off the pillow.

Astro flips the left page to Jack's mystery. In a single breath, he explains, "Jack completes his math homework and packs it away the same night. Early the next morning, Jack and Anna attend a program before class. Then, before Ms. White's homework check, it disappears. It's always his math, never his reading. He has a few friends and zero bullies. That's about it."

Astra nods, yawns again, and loses her fight with her pillow — letting her head fall and rest on the soft, cool pillowcase. "Astro," she mutters softly, feeling her eyelids fall. "Why can't we tell our friends that we helped people and solved mysteries before we moved?"

Astro narrows his eyes and furrows his eyebrows. Preparing himself for an argument, Astro glares at Astra and opens his mouth. But seeing her resting, he pauses. Instead, he exhales through his nose.

Realizing her genuine question — and the fact that she's barely awake — Astro softens his gaze. "Because I don't want to draw attention. I'm already nervous as it

★ THE SIBLINGS' DOUBLE TROUBLES ★

is. And I *definitely* don't want people knowing about our... talents," he softly explains, glancing over. "I mean, think about what you just did." He sighs. "If we don't have any other options, or they figure it out themselves, then fine. But remember, Mom and Dad want us to be careful."

Keeping her eyes shut, Astra hums quietly. Barely moving her lips, she mutters, "B-But they're nice, so we can probably trust these two."

A few seconds pass, and Astro says, "You know, just because someone's nice — or seems nice — does *not* mean they're trustworthy. That's going to get you in trouble one of these days."

Barely awake, she mumbles, "Then it's a good thing I have you here looking out for me."

He looks back over. "But —" Astro stops as he hears and sees his sister sleeping.

Thinking about Astra's comment, a soft, subtle smile spreads across his face. He flips to a page in the back of his notebook, writes inside, and puts it away. Afterward, he lowers the television volume and resumes the movie.

Later that afternoon, Astra wakes up just before their parents arrive home. They finish their evening together as a family.

— CHAPTER SEVEN —

Switch Siblings

During recess the next day, Astro and Anna pair up and walk to the far end of the swing set. Anna sits at the end. Sitting beside her, Astro places his notebook on his lap, and five minutes of silence pass.

Feeling his palms drowning in sweat, Astro fidgets with his fingers, trying to get a handle on his nerves. *Ack! What should I say first?* Astro thinks to himself. *Is she upset about yesterday? If she is, does she even want to talk to me? Agh! And if she isn't going to talk to me, she won't want to answer any of my questions!* Astro takes a deep breath.

"W-What color is your necklace?" Astro asks to test the water — since he already knows the answer.

Afraid of saying something wrong, Anna quickly answers, "G-Gold."

"Mm," he hums, watching her reach up toward her neck. "S-So, uh, A-Astra told me you got the necklace as

★ THE SIBLINGS' DOUBLE TROUBLES ★

a gift." He sees Anna nod. "C-Can you tell me more about what it looks like? I'm having a hard time picturing it."

Anna's posture pops up in her swing. "Oh! Okay, sure. So" — using hand motions — "picture a gold chain that connects in the back. Then, in the middle of the chain, opposite the latch, my name's written out."

"Ohh, I see! Thank you for using so much detail," he compliments. Starting to calm down, Astro opens his notebook and asks, "Do you remember if your necklace was tight around your neck? Or did it loop and sit on your chest? Or was it even longer?"

Anna thinks for a moment. "It *was* loopy. I-I'm not sure *how* loopy, but my name sat about" — pointing just beneath her collarbone — "here."

He looks over and nods. *Ah. Loose but not long. So, people definitely saw it since it wasn't underneath her clothes*, he thinks. *But who would want someone else's personalized necklace? Maybe another Anna?*

He jots inside his notebook and lifts his head. "Do you like running? Any sports?"

"I mean, I don't like running for fun," she says with a confused grin. "But sports are okay. I like the games we play in gym class. L-Like kickball and dodgeball. You know, that type of stuff. So I mainly like playing games and hanging out with friends."

Astro nods and narrows his eyes. "Any chance you remember the details of the chain pieces? Like, are they small or big? Round? Oval?"

"Um, I'm sorry. I don't really remember. I think they were small, but I'm not sure." She reaches up toward her neck again.

This time, Astro jumps on her action and asks, "Did you touch your necklace often?"

"Oh, a little bit. It was just a small habit I picked up. It really bothered Jack," she admits, putting her hand down in her lap. She sighs and shakes her head. "To be honest, I might reach for it more *now* than when I actually had it. But that probably sounds weird."

"Ahh. No, I don't think it's weird. I think it makes sense. If you miss something, it's only natural you reach for it more," he consoles. "Um, is there any chance you remember a place or time you had it last?"

"Um, n-no. I mean, not specifically."

"How about the opposite? When did you first realize it was missing?"

"It was a school day. I woke up and —"

"Wait," Astro interrupts, "sorry. Do you sleep with your necklace?"

"Yeah, usually. Um, but then I went into the bathroom to take a showerrr-uhh . . ." She tilts her head up and stares at the sky.

Hearing Anna's sudden pause, Astro looks over with a curious expression. "W-Were you saying shower?"

"Ew! What-No! Girls don't shower!" she spits out with rose-pink cheeks.

Astro grins, raises his eyebrows, and drops his chin. "Y-You don't . . . shower?"

Anna's eyes widen, and her face turns beet red. She covers her face and stammers for a response.

Seeing Anna fidget and flail in her swing, Astro feels slightly guilty for teasing her. Eventually, he says, "You *do* remember I have a sister, right?"

She pops up in her seat. "Oh . . . Ha! Yeah! A-And" — suspiciously glancing at Astro — "sh-she showers?"

Astro chuckles. "Yes, she showers."

"Okay, yeah! I was going to do that! But as I reached up to remove my necklace, it was gone," she continues explaining.

"Hmm... how interesting," he says, writing down her explanation. He squints and looks up at Anna. "You've checked your —"

"Bathroom? Room? House? Yes," she answers with a gentle nod.

"I figured," Astro says. "So, since you borrow your brother's homework —"

"But I put it back before he gets up!" she retorts to defend herself. "And most of the time, I only borrow it to check if our answers are matching! I swear!"

"I know, I know," Astro reassures, raising his hands and showing Anna his palms — as if revealing that he's not hiding anything. "Is there any chance your necklace fell off into his backpack?"

"Oh, s-sorry," Anna apologizes, taking a breath. "I-I don't think so. I *have* looked, but it wasn't there."

Astro nods. "Well, while we're talking about Jack — and I'm not accusing you of anything — do you have any ideas about where his homework is going?"

"Honestly? I have no clue," she says with a sigh. "But it's so" — shaking her head — "frustrating. Because now everyone thinks he's stupi — ahh, not smart. Or that he doesn't care about school. But none of that's true!"

"Yeah. Last week, Jack said something about people thinking he's a slacker?"

"Right. But I don't think he knows about that other stuff, so please don't tell him. It'll just make him more upset."

"Okay. Well, I think I have everything I nee —"

"Ms. White's class! Please line up for lunch!" calls the recess monitor — unknowingly interrupting Astro.

"Good timing!" jokes Anna.

Astro smiles. "Uh, just like I planned?"

With a few chuckles, they lift themselves off their swings and walk to the opposite end of the swing set toward their siblings.

☆ ☆ ☆ ☆

Astra and Jack break off and stroll to the end of the swing set closest to the blacktop.

Astra watches Jack's movements as they approach the end of the swings. *Hm. Seems a bit tense,* she thinks, watching Jack walk and sit down in the swing — leaving the end seat free. *There's nothing like a good laugh to help ease the tension.*

Astra stands before him, bows, and extends her arm. Using an exaggerated British accent, she says, "Why, it's a pleasure to make you acquaintance, good sir." She lifts her head and gives a cheeky smile.

Looking both entertained and embarrassed, Jack grins. "Y-You too?"

Content with herself, she skips over to the available swing. *Maybe swinging will help him relax,* she thinks, pushing off the ground. Swaying enough to create a short but comfortable breeze, she takes a deep breath.

"So!" blurts Astra, catching Jack by surprise. "Someone's taking your homework, huh? Who would want *math equations* of all things?" She giggles at the sound of her ridiculous question.

Jack smiles and suggests, "Someone who likes math, I guess." He takes a few steps back on the swing and lifts his feet off the ground to start swinging.

She grins and asks, "Who's on your suspect list?"

"Well, *I* thought it was Anna. So if it's *not* her, I-I have no idea. Someone who likes making my life hard! That's who!" he jokes with a chuckle.

"Yeah! You got *that* right!" she agrees. "So what do you do after school? What's your usual routine?"

★ THE SIBLINGS' DOUBLE TROUBLES ★

"I go home. And sometimes I grab a snack. Then, I start my homework with something playing in the background. Like music or movies. Then —"

"Wait. Where do you do your homework?"

"Either in the living room or my bedroom. I guess it depends on the day. Lately, it's been my room. But then I eat dinner, spend time with my parents, and I go to sleep," he explains. Jack slouches over and drags his feet in the dusty pebbles to stop his swing.

Astra stops swinging. "Oh no! What's wrong?"

"It's just . . . I haven't been spending that much time with Anna," he murmurs with a shaky, quivering voice. "Y-Y'know, with the homework and necklace stuff, we don't spend time together like we used to. A-And I — Well, I'm afraid I've ruined our relationship with each other."

Hearing his voice tremble, Astra feels his sadness, and her eyes begin to tear up. She squeezes her eyes shut and forces herself to turn away — to keep herself from being engulfed in his emotions.

Do I respond to his feelings? Or should I ask why they haven't made up? Astra takes a few deep breaths and regains her composure. Looking back at Jack, she sees him slumping over, nearly falling off his swing. *His feelings,* she decides.

"Jack," Astra says tenderly. "When Astro and I are fighting —"

Jack scoffs with a sniffle. "That's hard to imagine."

"As hard as it may be, it happens," she says, slightly irritated by his remark. "And when we *are*, our parents usually remind us of something pretty important."

Jack continues his disbelief. "And what's that?"

"First, they normally say that relationships can be some of the most complex things in the world."

Jack chuckles again — this time with a subtle nod. "Yeah, that sounds about right."

"Then they tell us that they can be some of the most fragile things," she says, seeing Jack sigh. "But they can also be the most robust."

"What's that? Is that a fancy robot?"

"No. It means strong," Astra says, watching Jack gulp and eat his words. A few seconds later, she comments, "After getting to know you two, I have a feeling that you can mend what's been broken."

Jack sniffles, coughs, and glances away from Astra. Using his left hand, he dries his eyes and says, "Maybe

★ THE SIBLINGS' DOUBLE TROUBLES ★

the person stealing my homework is the same person who stole Anna's necklace."

"Mm ... I'm sorry, but I'm not sure that's going to be the case."

"No, don't be sorry," he reassures with a smile. "I'm just grasping at straws. I really don't know what to do now. Oh! Before I forget, thank you for helping us with our problems."

Jack gently pushes off the ground and swings again.

Astra joins him. "So, you complete your homework at home. I don't think *Anna's* taking it. *You're* obviously not stealing from yourself. And I doubt your *parents* are taking —" Astra stops her swing and stares at the sky with a puzzled expression. "WAIT! Your *parents* aren't taking your homewor —"

"No! Astra! What?" he questions, grinning and shaking his head.

Astra blushes and shrugs. "Okay, okay! I just thought I'd make sure," she reasons, pumping her legs to swing again.

"I don't think that's something you need to check in most cases," he says with a brief chuckle.

"Yeah, you're right, you're right," she agrees, feeling the conversation lighten. "So do your friends copy your homework?"

"Nah. I only have a few. But they're usually good about completing their own work. Plus, they'd probably ask Anna for that type of stuff, not me."

"Yeah, true," she agrees before widening her eyes and stopping her swing. "Not that you only have a few friends! I-I meant the homework part!"

Jack smiles. "Don't worry. I know what you meant."

With a sigh of relief, she continues swinging. "Do you put your name on your homework?"

"Of course! It's almost always the first thing I do!"

Astra grumbles playfully. "I think I'm out of — Oh! Is anyone picking on you?" she asks casually, watching him out of the corner of her eye.

"Yeah! Whoever's stealing my math homework!" he exaggerates, laughing at his own joke.

Astra flashes an amused grin. *Hmm, a funny answer to a serious question? Is he using humor to cover an honest response?* She watches Jack use Anna's strategy and fake a smile.

Dragging her shoes through the pebbles, she stops her swing. Astra tilts her head down and raises her eyebrows. "Are you sure?" she asks, staring into Jack's eyes.

Jack follows Astra and stops his swing. He releases a heavy sigh and explains, "It's complicated. I'm not being *bullied,* per se . . ."

Astra doesn't say anything. Instead, she gives him a warm, gentle smile.

"Well, me and Anna go to a before-school program. And we usually play gym games."

"Oo! That sounds fun!"

"Yeah, it is!" he agrees. "But there's this group. And they're kind of mean during the games. Tsh" — looking to the side — "they're kind of mean all the time."

Astra furrows her eyebrows. "Oh. Less fun now that you said that."

"Yeah," Jack murmurs. "Oh! But Anna's not scared of them." A content grin spreads across his face. "She goes out of her way to be the rain on their parade. Sometimes she even wins!"

"Oh, yeah?" Astra asks, grinning and raising an eyebrow. "What kind of rain?"

Jack's eyebrows dance, and his grin morphs into a smirk. "Oh, I'm talking thunderstorm." They laugh at themselves before Jack admits, "It's awesome that she tries her best and gives it everything she has."

"Aw, that's so sweet! We've gotta tell her!" Astra gets up from her swing.

"Yeah. Wait, what? No, no, no, no, no, no!" Jack declines, frantically shaking his head from side to side.

Astra sits back down and playfully purses her lips. *"Booo."*

"Ms. White's class! Please line up for lunch!" calls the recess monitor.

Getting up from their seats, they notice their siblings heading over and wait for them to catch up.

They all walk to the blacktop without talking about the mysteries.

The hall monitor leads the class toward the building. The Seeker siblings straggle a few feet behind everyone to update one another about the mysteries.

The rest of the school day, Astro feels distracted. No matter how hard he tries not to, he can't help but twirl the two mysteries around in the back of his mind. Spinning on the cases, Astro nearly has gold strings pouring from his ears.

— CHAPTER EIGHT —

The Vivid Visions

Caught up in his thoughts, Astro saunters into their home after school. Pondering the cases, he slips his shoes off, ambles to the living room, and plops onto the couch.

☆ ☆ ☆ ☆

Though Astra notices Astro in a daze, there's only one thing on her mind as she runs through the doorway. Throwing herself onto her favorite couch in the living room, she eagerly stares at Astro.

Feeling an excitement welling up inside her soul, like opening a secret present at Christmas time, Astra can't help but squirm around on the cushions.

Watching her zombie-like brother sit on the opposite couch and stare off into space, she scowls at the lack of attention. A cheeky grin spreads across her face. She

★ THE SEEKER SIBLINGS ★

gets up, walks over, and plops down beside him. With a massive grin and starstruck eyes, she slowly leans in toward his right cheek.

Astro shifts his eyes and sees her a few inches from his face. With a blank expression, he asks, "Are you that excited about homework?"

"Yeah! Wait, what? NO! Are you" — making her eyebrows bounce — "going to do . . . the thing?"

Astro gulps. "The . . . what?"

"You know," she baits, backing away from his face. "I know you've been thinking about it."

Astro lightly closes his eyes. "The . . . visions?"

"The visions! So? Are you? Huh?" — wiggling left and right, nudging his arm — "Huh? Huh?"

Seeing Astra so animated, a grin escapes his lips as her excitement begins rubbing off on him.

He pulls out his special notebook and places it on the coffee table. "*After* our homework," emphasizes Astro, "which one did you want to do first?"

"Jack's! No, Anna's! No, Jack's! Yeah, let's do Jack's!"

Astro flips to Jack's mystery page, and Astra returns to the other couch. They begin their homework.

☆ ☆ ☆ ☆

★ THE SIBLINGS' DOUBLE TROUBLES ★

Stepping off their school bus, Jack and Anna head toward their house. Several meters of space continue to separate them.

Strolling on the cream-colored sidewalk, Jack stares at the concrete. He can't stop hearing Astra's voice inside his head. *Relationships can be complex things. They can be fragile. But they can also be the most robust.* Jack looks up from the sidewalk and sees Anna walking in front of him. He stares at the back of her head. Astra's voice continues repeating. *You can mend what's been broken.*

Closing in on their house, Jack starts thinking about Astra's remarks. *Mend what's been broken. Can I really? Can I fix the things that are broken? What if it's too late? What if Anna doesn't want to make up with me?* He sighs. *I guess I'll never know if I don't try.*

Hesitantly, Jack opens his mouth to call out to his sister. "A —" His voice gets trapped inside his throat, and he clears it a few times as Anna enters their house. Jack rolls his eyes at himself. *Oh, yeah. Great job,* he thinks sarcastically. *I'm sure she heard that.*

Following her through the doorway and into the house, he closes the door behind them.

Anna quickly slips her shoes off and vanishes down the hallway toward her room.

"ANNA!" Jack blurts out impulsively, standing with one shoe off.

Anna's head pops out from around the corner with a curious expression. "Y-Yes, Jack?"

"Er-Oh! Uh, w-well, um," he stammers, feeling his palms sweat, "d-did you want some water?" Jack gulps.

Anna's eyebrows twitch. "Oh. Um, no. Not really," she declines before disappearing again.

With light-pink cheeks, Jack rubs his forehead and removes his other shoe. *Water? Really?* Jack shakes his head and sighs. *I should've at least offered her orange juice,* he cracks, attempting to cheer himself up from his massive failure.

Jack enters his room, sits at his desk, and starts his homework.

☆ ☆ ☆ ☆

With their homework assignments complete, Astro and Astra pack their school materials away. Astra pauses the movie, and Astro slides his notebook closer.

★ THE SIBLINGS' DOUBLE TROUBLES ★

The twins concentrate on the two mystery pages and fill in any missing details — one mystery at a time. After adding everything they can remember, Astro flips back to Jack's page. He scans the page for nearly ten minutes, reviewing the information slowly and methodically.

Instruction Page

Optional Activity!

The following pages will include the Seeker siblings' notes about the mystery. Feel free to keep mental notes and continue reading. However, you can also write down your thoughts and/or make notes as the mystery unfolds!

Note: If this book is **NOT** your personal copy, please use a separate sheet of paper or a notebook.

If this book **IS** your personal copy, you're welcome to write inside these pages! You can also use a separate sheet of paper or notebook!

IMPORTANT: I recommend using a pencil to write in your book. Using ink may lead to bleeding through pages!

Follow either instruction set below.

1. Read the mystery information.
2. Fill out the theories and speculations section, then create your own ideas and plans.
3. When you finish the book, decide whether or not your theories, speculations, and plans would've been successful.

- OR –

1. Continue reading and fill out the sections as you learn more information to keep your own record of the mystery.

Above all, enjoy reading, and have
fun watching the mystery unfold!

- Jack -

Mystery: Stolen Math Worksheets.

Facts:
- Writes his name on his homework.
- Completes homework at night.
- Places homework in his folder, then in his backpack.
- Sometimes Anna copies (but returns to his bag).
- They leave early in the morning.
- Missing worksheet during the homework check.
- Always has his reading homework (reading log).
- Attends a program before school.

Opinions:
- Suspects his sister, Anna. Anna denies stealing.
- The students believe he's a lazy slacker.

Feelings:
- Is scared of a group before school.
- Admires Anna for trying her best at everything.
- Wishes they could spend more time together.
- Afraid he's ruined his relationship with Anna.

Who is Jack?
- Nice, outgoing, and friendly. Hard worker.
- Likes his sister, though he might not say it to her.

- Jack -

Theories + Speculations (Guesses):

_____

_____

_____

_____

_____

Plan:

_____

_____

_____

_____

Solutions + Results:

_____

_____

_____

_____

_____

★ THE SEEKER SIBLINGS ★

After reading his notes, Astro closes his eyes and slowly exhales. Picturing Jack in his head, Astro thinks about his habits and personality. Considering the different facts, opinions, and details, Astro starts painting a scenario inside his head. He dives deeper into his vision.

Astro pictures a generic bedroom with Jack sitting at an ordinary desk. He watches Jack place his homework inside his school folder. Astro sees him lean over and slide his folder into his backpack.

Staring at the backpack, Astro speeds up his vision to the following morning. Jack grabs his bag, slings it over his right shoulder, and exits the bedroom.

Fast forwarding again, he sees Jack hop out of a generic car and walk up to school. But as he enters the main entrance, the vision warps into a cloudy, murky mess. It fades, leaving Astro alone in a black void.

Astro opens his eyes, returning to the living room.

"So?" asks Astra. "See anything? Anything interesting?"

Astro quickly says, "Jack placed his finished homework inside his bag. The next morning, he grabbed it and went to school. But the vision faded as he walked through the entrance."

"So he must be losing his homework sometime between home and class, right?"

"Yeah. Probably at the school program. My guess is someone's taking it while Jack's distracted."

"Really? Who?"

Astro dips an eyebrow. "W-Well, I didn't see *that*. But if we're doing Anna's mystery" — flipping to her mystery page — "we need to hurry."

"C'mon baby, give me the finds!"

Astro scrunches his nose and frowns in disgust. Looking up from his notebook, he sees Astra closing her eyes and twitching her eyebrows.

Astra clears her throat and says, "I, uh, I apologize. That . . . that sounded cringe. Was it cringe? Tell me it wasn't cringe."

He gestures to the page with his right hand. "Should I?"

"Y-Yes, please." Astra drops her blushing face into her hands and shakes her head.

Like before, Astro scans through the mystery page. He reviews the information slowly and methodically.

- Anna -

Mystery: Stolen Necklace.

Facts:
- Received the necklace for her last birthday.
- Gold-colored with "Anna" as the nameplate.
- Sits just below her collarbone.
- She usually sleeps with it on.
- Realized it was missing during her morning routine.
- Spends a lot of time at home and at school.
- Enjoys playing group gym games.
- Attends a program before school.

Opinions:
- Suspects her brother, Jack. Jack denies stealing.
- Anna believes someone has taken it.

Feelings:
- Upset, deflated, sad.
- Could feel guilty about losing such a special gift.
- Desperate to locate her necklace.
- Frustrated that everyone thinks Jack's a slacker.

Who is Anna?
- Competitive, fiery, and friendly. Protective.
- Tries her hardest/best with everything.

- Anna -

Theories + Speculations (Guesses):

Plan:

Solutions + Results:

Closing his eyes, Astro exhales and pictures Anna. He thinks about her habits and personality. Considering the various facts, opinions, and details, he paints another scenario inside his mind. Slowly, Astro dives deeper into his vision.

He pictures a plain room with a bed. Astro imagines Anna waking up and tossing the covers off herself as she gets up. Anna walks out of the room and into a hallway. Astro joins her as she enters an empty generic bathroom. The bathroom has a shower, a toilet, and a sink. A mirror is mounted on the wall over the countertop.

Astro stands in the doorway and watches Anna. She stops before the countertop and rubs her eyes. Leaning in toward the mirror, Anna stares at her neck and gasps. Astro sees her reach up for her necklace — like he saw at the swing set — as panic washes over her face.

Dashing out of the bathroom, Anna sprints back to the bedroom. Astro follows, and he sees her frantically throw blankets and pillows off her bed.

"Stop," Astro whispers out loud, pausing the vision and freezing Anna in the middle of her crazy search. He rewinds the vision and places her back in bed. Looking closer, Astro notices her sleeping without her necklace.

★ THE SIBLINGS' DOUBLE TROUBLES ★

Astro furrows his eyebrows. *It's not around her neck, and neither Jack nor her parents stole it,* thinks Astro. *If it's not in her house . . . did it ever come back?* The vision turns into a foggy mess and disappears. Once again, he's alone in a dark void. Astro opens his eyes and returns to the living room.

"So? So?" Astra questions, having recovered from her previous embarrassment. "What did you see? Who took it?"

He sighs and says, "I'm not sure. I didn't see much. But I *do* have some ideas on how to narrow down the mysteries."

"Really! What are they?"

He shakes his head. "Nope, sorry. I'll tell you when I tell Jack and Anna tomorrow."

She purses her lips and frowns. *"Boooo!"*

Astro grins and writes down his speculations and theories inside his notebook. He also adds his plans for each mystery.

As he finishes writing his last sentence, Astro's eyes tire, and his vision blurs.

Thump! Thump! Thump! Astro's head begins pounding, matching the rhythm of his heartbeat. As his head throbs and pounds, a sharp pain squeezes Astro's skull.

Feeling his eyes starting to ache, Astro closes them and reaches up to hold his head.

"A-Astra!" he winces.

"I'm on it," Astra replies, jumping up from the couch and bolting to the nearby bathroom. She slides Astro's designated drawer open and quickly locates his medication. Grabbing his prescription and a small cup of water, she carefully but swiftly returns to the living room.

Handing Astro his medicine and water, she watches him swallow the pill and lie down.

Recovering for the rest of the evening, Astro relaxes and recuperates. As usual, Astro eats dinner and spends quality time with his family. However, today, he returns to his bedroom earlier than usual to prepare for the next day — and to get enough rest.

— CHAPTER NINE —

Paving the Plans

Before class Wednesday morning, the Seeker siblings wait for their friends by Astra's desk.

Seeing Jack and Anna stroll through the doorway, Astra subtly waves them down.

While Jack and Anna walk toward the Seeker duo, Astro grabs his notebook. He holds it by the spine. Letting gravity do its thing, he sees the cover separate itself from the other pages. As it falls and pulls away, it reveals a small piece of paper between the cover and the first page. He grabs the slip of paper with one hand and squeezes his notebook shut with the other. A small puff of air blows onto his face. Astro sets his notebook down on Astra's desk and glances at the paper.

Time	HW (Y/N)
5:30 a.m	
6:30 a.m.	
7:30 a.m.	
8:30 a.m.	

"Good morning," greets Jack.

"Morning," Astro says while handing him the piece of paper. "If you'd check your bag for your homework at these times, that'd be great. But other than that, please, do NOT change your usual routine."

Jack grabs the paper, glances at it, and nods. "Okay, sure! Oh! But" — sticking the paper in his pocket — "I was thinking. Maybe someone's copying my homework and throwing it away! So if we can't figure out *who's* taking it, we could try figuring out where it *ends up.*"

Trying his hardest to keep from making a confused expression, Astro lightly closes his eyes and furrows his eyebrows. "Uh, it's... er-it's a... thought," he says, trying to be supportive. "But" — opening his eyes and looking at Anna — "why did you return the worksheet after you borrowed it?"

Anna's eyes widen as she looks at the ceiling and raises her voice as high as it will go. "Ahhh," she squeals for a couple of seconds before exhaling and returning her voice to normal. "Because I didn't need it anymore."

"Right, because you had your own," he says, turning back to his friend. "Jack. It's risky enough to steal someone else's homework. It's even more so if they steal it, copy it, and then return it or throw it away."

"What? B-But Anna's done it several times."

"Uh, not *copied*," Anna clarifies defensively.

Jack exhales. "O-Okay. Steal and return."

Astro nods. "Right. But that's at your house. Not at school where everyone can see you. And 'several times' is different than every day," he explains.

"Oh, r-right," he says, thinking about the paper in his pocket. "Well, I guess we'll know *when* it goes missing if I fill this out, right?"

Astro nods again, deciding to take the partial win. "Right. And if you can't check at the exact times, just check when you can and write it down. But try not to skip any completely. And make sure you physically see your homework sitting in your folder."

"Yeah, yeah! I got it. I got it."

★ THE SEEKER SIBLINGS ★

"Okay, okay," he says, backing off and turning to Anna. "And this" — reaching into his pocket — "is for you." Grinning and lifting his hand from his pocket, a multicolored paperclip necklace swings in front of their faces.

Anna's jaw drops. "Aww, whaat?" she whines before pursing her lips and adding, "That is so not cute!"

"Yeah, yeah," he says. "But cute or not, this is your new necklace. Go ahead and treat this one as if it's your gold one. Don't change *anything*. Take it off and put it on whenever you want. Heck. You can do whatever you want with it. Just make sure to treat this like your gold necklace. Got it?"

"G-Got it," she says, sighing and accepting the necklace. "B-But no one's going to want this one. So how are we going to catch the thief?"

Astro holds a wink with a nonchalant shrug. "I guess we'll just have to wait and see."

"Ah, jeez," she groans, blushing and putting on the ridiculous paperclip necklace. "Oh!" — raising her eyebrows — "Actually, it's almost the same size as the gold one! I mean, it's not *perfect*. But it's close."

★ THE SIBLINGS' DOUBLE TROUBLES ★

"Well, fantastic! I handcrafted it myself. My blood, sweat, and tears went into it," he says with a content grin. "But not literally. It was just an expressio —"

"No, Astro," Astra interrupts, scratching her forehead in embarrassment. "I think she got it."

Anna giggles.

"O-Oh, right," he says, rubbing the back of his head. "A-Anyway . . . hopefully, we'll get a better idea of your situations with these plans."

Jack and Anna nod in agreement.

Astro grabs his notebook, and the boys head to their seats as class begins for the day.

Unbeknownst to Anna, the Seeker twins observe her throughout the day. Their eyes follow her around the classroom, in the hallways, at recess, lunch, and everything in between. Astra even keeps an eye on her during their bathroom breaks.

Woo! Woo! Woo! Woo! The final bell rings, and the Seeker siblings exit their classroom. They end the school day without any more information, clues, or leads.

Astro and Astra enter their home. Instead of playing a movie and working in the living room, they retire to their bedrooms to begin their homework. While they

★ THE SEEKER SIBLINGS ★

work, Astro and Astra battle with their feelings of hopelessness, disappointment, and uncertainty.

After finishing his homework, Astro moves from his desk to his bed. He sits in the center of his bed, starts a movie, and thinks about Jack and Anna.

Knock. Knock.

Hearing the knock, Astro closes his eyes and drops his shoulders. Leaning back, he bounces on the mattress. Grabbing the remote, Astro pushes a button and pauses the movie at the three-minute mark.

"Come in," Astro says, readjusting and leaning back against his headboard.

Astra opens the door, crosses his room, and sits at his desk on the opposite wall. "So I've been thinking."

"Oh? How'd that feee . . ." Astro notices Astra glaring at him with an unamused face, and his voice trails off into a throat clear. "What were you thinking about?"

"It's just . . ." Astra exhales. "What are our chances of solving both of these mysteries?"

Turning onto his left side, Astro faces her and thinks for a few seconds. "The odds of figuring out Jack's problem are good. But finding out who took a little necklace that's been missing for several weeks? It's . . . unlikely," he admits.

★ THE SIBLINGS' DOUBLE TROUBLES ★

Astra deflates like a punctured balloon and sinks into the chair. Unable to slump further, she turns into a puddle and slides off the chair onto the floor.

Lying on her back, Astra says, "It just seems like we're missing something."

"Hopefully, they'll bring us more information tomorrow," he says. "Jack has his instructions, and Anna's getting used to living with a necklace again."

"Yeah," she agrees from the ground. "But it feels like we could be doing more, you know?"

Astro's eyelids and eyebrows twitch. "Er-we're doing quite a bit already, aren't we —"

"But more!"

"Like what?" he grumbles.

"I don't know! You're the smart one! Come up with something!"

"What more can we do? We can only *do* so much!" he snaps. "What do you want me to say? It's not like we can go and —" Astro's eyes light up, and he pops up from his mattress.

Hearing the sudden pause, Astra jerks her head up from the ground and snaps it toward Astro. "What?" she shouts, sitting up. "What is it?"

Smiling and running his fingers through his black and white hair, he says, "I can't believe I didn't think of this sooner! But I've got another idea!"

"WHAT? Tell me! What is it?"

Astro turns and lets his legs hang over the side of his bed.

After filling Astra in on his idea, they lie on his bed and continue the movie.

Later that evening, Astro and Astra join their parents in the living room.

Without warning, Astro says, "Mom, Dad. Can I ask you something?"

"You just did!" Mr. Seeker says with a smirk.

Mrs. Seeker looks at her husband, raises an eyebrow, and loosely shakes her head. Trying to keep from smiling, she turns back to Astro. "What did you want to ask, sweetie?"

"S-So there's this program before school, and some of our classmates —"

"CAN WE GO?" blurts Astra. "Just for a day or two! Please?"

Silence fills the air before Mr. Seeker says, "But you don't really need to go, do you?"

"Of course we do!" argues Astra. "Please!"

★ THE SIBLINGS' DOUBLE TROUBLES ★

Mrs. Seeker squints. "Why do you *need* to go?"

Astra's eyes widen. "Oh-ah. H-How *else* are we supposed to make friends?"

Their parents exchange suspicious looks.

"Pretty please!" Astra begs, clapping her hands with her fingers pointing toward the ceiling. She strenuously pushes her hands against each other, making her arms and hands vibrate back and forth.

After several moments, Mr. Seeker admits, "Hm . . . I suppose it wouldn't hurt for a day. I'll call tomorrow to see if you two can visit on Friday. Does that work?"

"Yay!" Astra celebrates, running and jumping on Mr. Seeker to give him a hug. "Thank you, Dad!"

Astro nods and grins at their squished dad. "Y-Yes, thank you!"

That night in their beds, the Seeker siblings lie restless underneath their covers. Though they have another plan in motion, they hope Jack and Anna bring them more information tomorrow.

— CHAPTER TEN —

The Missing Information

Waiting by Astra's desk, the Seeker siblings fidget with their fingers and stare at the doorway in anticipation. After a few students pass through, Jack and Anna rush into the room.

"Astro! Astra!" Jack shouts, waving the small piece of paper in his hand. "Good news! It was —"

"Shhhh," Astro hushes gently. "Remember, our help is a secret."

"Oh! Oops," he says, lowering his voice to a whisper. "The math homework was taken between seven-thirty and eight-thirty! But I don't get how that helps. Sure, we know *when* it's being stolen. But we still don't know who's stealing it."

Astro sits down at Astra's desk. "Well, what did you do between seven-thirty and eight-thirty this morning?" he asks, opening his notebook.

★ THE SIBLINGS' DOUBLE TROUBLES ★

Jack's eyes light up. "OH!" he says excitedly before his eyes dim, and he deflates. "Oh. Like *everything*. We came to school a few minutes before seven-thirty."

"For the before-school program?" Astro clarifies as he writes in his notebook.

"Yeah! Then I hung my backpack on their movable coatrack and —"

"Movable coatrack?"

"Yeah." He chuckles. "It has wheels. Y'know, so they can move it in and out of the gym. I-I don't know why I thought you needed to know that." He shakes his head in embarrassment. "J-Just — Never mind."

"Ah-okay."

Jack continues, "After I hung up my bag, I checked for my homework. Then —"

"And it was there?" he asks, raising his eyes from his notebook.

Jack nods. "And then we ate breakfast and got back a little after eight. For gym time, they let everyone shoot basketballs. Around eight-thirty, everyone left the gym for their classes. So on our way over, I checked for my homework, and it was gone."

Astro finishes his notetaking before putting one of his hands up. "Wait, stop. You *both* ate breakfast?"

"Yeah."

"At school?" Astro clarifies.

"Yeah."

"Does everyone?"

"No. If you don't want — or need — to eat breakfast, you have to stay in the gym."

Astro grins, shakes his head, and writes in his notebook.

Astra notices Anna's spirit deflating. *Aw, I'm sure it's difficult watching the progress they're making with Jack's mystery,* Astra thinks. *I should say something.*

"Bestie!" squeals Astra. "I see you still have your necklace!"

Anna gives a cheeky grin and exaggerates, "But of course! I've been treasuring this *once-in-a-lifetime piece of jewelry.*"

"That's my girl!" she praises, high-fiving Anna.

Keeping his eyes down in his notebook, Astro scowls and calls, "Anna."

Anna jumps, and her body stiffens. "Oop! Ah, yes?"

Astro looks up and gives a gentle smile. "I-It's just me," he reassures. "Do you normally play basketball in the morning?"

★ THE SIBLINGS' DOUBLE TROUBLES ★

Anna chuckles and relaxes. "Right. Um, usually we play a group game like dodgeball, kickball, or something like that. But I think we got back late today, so they gave us some free gym time instead."

"I see. I-I'm sorry, but I don't know who took your necklace yet."

Anna slowly sighs through her nose, trying to hide her disappointment. "That . . . that's okay," she says with a twitching smile.

Astra watches Anna's shoulders drop. "Don't worry, bestie!" she consoles. "We haven't given up yet! Right, Astro?"

"Right," he reassures, with a nod.

Anna feels her eyes starting to water and looks up at the ceiling to keep her tears from falling.

"Continue doing what you're doing," Astro encourages. "Remember to treat this necklace like your gold one. Do whatever you need to do to trick yourself into believing this is your gold necklace."

Anna sniffles. "O-Okay," she says, wiping a tear from her eye. "W-We *are still trying to find it,* right?"

"Aw, bestie. I promise we're still searching for it," Astra comforts, giving Anna a hug. "And I swear we'll let you know when we're out of ideas, okay?"

★ THE SEEKER SIBLINGS ★

Hugging Astra, Anna repeatedly nods on her friend's shoulder. After calming down, she lets go, and a determined expression washes over her face.

Anna wipes her eyes and takes a final sniffle. "I'll do whatever it takes!" she declares.

Soon after, they all break off from their small circle and sit in their assigned seats.

Copying the previous day, the Seeker siblings watch Anna. Specifically, they stare at the paperclip necklace hanging around her neck.

Woo! Woo! Woo! Woo! The final bell rings. School ends without any further information.

After school, Astro pauses at the family computer while Astra plops down on her usual couch to find a movie. By the time she starts one, Astro is sitting on the other couch with his homework. Nearly an hour later, they finish their homework assignments and grab some snacks for their next movie.

"Astro?" chirps Astra, tossing her head back against the couch.

Astro raises his eyebrows and looks over with a mouthful of crackers. "Hm?"

"I've been thinking about Anna's necklace," she says, watching Astro nod. "I'm just wondering if you had any ideas about who took it. It's just — I don't really get the paperclip necklace deal. And it doesn't really seem like we're doing anything to find the thief, much less catch them."

Astro sits with food in his mouth and stares at the television. Keeping his facial muscles still, he tries swallowing but chokes and breaks into a tiny coughing fit.

Astra gasps. "What is it?" she questions, ignoring the flying cracker pieces. "You *gotta* tell me *now*. I know you know something!"

Astro grabs his glass of water and takes several gulps. Catching his breath, he sighs, realizing he isn't going to get past his sister. "Fine. But it's something you have to keep secret. Got it?"

"Sure, sure!" she agrees with a ditzy, playful tone. "Now, pretty please, tell little ol' me!"

Astro narrows his eyes and furrows his eyebrows. "Promise?"

Astra freezes and considers the weight of her next words, especially with Astro. In a serious tone, she says, "I promise."

Astro takes a deep breath and says, "Okay. So, Anna doesn't know when she last had her necklace. She's already spent time looking around her house —"

"Right! I know that already," Astra interrupts with a puzzled expression.

Astro closes his eyes and tilts his head toward his left shoulder. "Okaaay." He starts again. "But if it's not at her house, and her family didn't take it, then —"

"Someone *else* must have taken it!" she says, cutting her brother off again.

Astro sits in silence and stares at Astra with a deadpan gaze. "Oh, *really?* Who?" he asks, growing annoyed by her interruptions.

"Huh? What do you mean? That's what we're trying to figure out!"

Astro sighs. "But think," he says, tapping his temple, "how hard would it be for someone to steal a necklace that someone's wearing?"

"I mean, it's possib —"

"*Without* letting them see you. *And* without having them remember who you are."

"Ahh-oh." She sighs, realizing the odds are shrinking. "A-Almost impossible. So what does that mean?"

"My guess?" he says, pausing and raising an eyebrow. "No one actually took it. Instead —"

"What! How is that possible?"

★ THE SIBLINGS' DOUBLE TROUBLES ★

"But" — raising his voice — *"instead,"* he says, growing even more irritated. "I'm guessing that Anna set it down somewhere and —"

"WHAT!"

"Shhh! Astra! Please!" he snaps.

"Oops, I-I'm sorry! I'm just excited!"

He shakes his head. "Remember, you can't tell Anna anything, or it will affect the results!"

"Yeah, I won't, I won't!" she reassures. "But wait. What results are you talking about?"

Astro grins and opens his notebook. Raising one of his eyebrows, he explains, "From our notes, we know Anna spends a lot of time at school and at home. Since she's already searched her house, I think there's a high chance it's somewhere at school. So I'm watching her and waiting to see if she puts it down somewhere."

"But why can't we tell —"

"Because if you *tell her,* then Anna will focus on it, and her actions won't be the same."

Astra flashes a look of confusion. "Her actions?"

"Right. If Anna's thinking about it, it's likely she'll set it down in a random spot or won't set it down at all."

"Ohh, I think I get it," says Astra. "So we're hoping she sets it down in the same spot as her real necklace?"

Astro smiles. "Exactly! Anna's unknowingly retracing her steps. And hopefully, we'll find —"

"Wait! But — Oh, oops!" she says, putting her hands over her mouth. "Sorry!"

"No, it's okay. What is it?"

"How do you know she won't place it down in a different spot? And how do we know someone didn't take it *after* she set it down? Oh! And how do you know they didn't go to a park or something and lose it *there* instead of at school."

Astro sighs and closes his eyes. "W-Well, I don't. And we won't know anything more until she sets it down. But hopefully, to keep it safe, she set it down somewhere that's hidden. I mean, this is a long shot, but it's my best idea."

Astra sighs and sprawls across the couch on her stomach. Planting her face into the cushion, she says, "HM-MPH-HMPH-HRM-MH!"

"What was that?" Astro asks. "You had some cushion in your face."

Astra lifts her face an inch off of the couch. "THIS SUCKS! She's so sad!" she yells, smacking her face back down into the cushion.

★ THE SIBLINGS' DOUBLE TROUBLES ★

Hearing the smacking sound, Astro silently giggles through his nose. But seeing Astra continuing to mimic a plank of wood, he dips his eyebrows.

"But, hey," he says softly, "we're getting a bit closer to solving Jack's missing homework problem. So that's good, right?"

Astra rolls onto her side. "Yeah. But I want to solve both of them! A perfect score! A win for each of us!"

"I mean, we still *could*," says Astro, trying to cheer her up. "But let's just focus on getting plenty of rest tonight since we might have to get up early."

Astra sits up and grabs a few crackers. "Wow! I'm surprised you remembered."

"What? My memory's not *that* bad."

Astra's eyes bounce around the room as her eyebrows twitch. "Ahh-right. Anyway, I *am* glad we don't have to go every day. I need my beauty sleep!"

"Oh, is *that* how it works?"

"Of course!" Astra exclaims before curling her lips into a mischievous smile. "Speaking of which, make sure to get plenty of hours tonight!"

Astro lightly smacks his lips and lets out a soft popping sound. "Are you calling me ugly?"

Astra blinks rapidly and stares at him with a derpy smile. *"Hmm? I don't know, am I?"*

His eyes narrow, and he lets out a big smirk. "Phew! Only a few *hours. You* could sleep for a few *weeks, and you'd still need —*"

Gasping and whipping her head at Astro, she warns, "You better not!"

Debating whether or not he should finish his quip, Astro gulps. After a few seconds, he says, "Right."

Astra lets out a cutesy giggle and reaches for another cracker.

As early evening approaches, the garage door hums softly. Hearing the low hum, Astro and Astra lock eyes and quickly jump up from the couches. They rush to the door leading to the garage and wait for their parents. A few seconds later, the door swings open.

"Good news!" Mr. Seeker shouts, hitting the garage door opener and stepping inside the house. "Guess who gets to attend the program tomorrow?"

"What! Really? Thanks, Dad!" squeals Astra, jumping up and giving him a big bear hug.

Astro goes in for a standard hug. "Thank you, Dad!"

★ THE SIBLINGS' DOUBLE TROUBLES ★

Mrs. Seeker grins and closes the door. "Let's try to arrive around seven. Your dad and I need to take care of some paperwork."

Astro and Astra nod in agreement.

The rest of the evening, the Seeker family spends quality time together. They eat dinner, watch a movie, and start a puzzle.

Eventually, the Seeker twins return to their rooms and get ready for bed. They fall asleep early to prepare for the following day.

— CHAPTER ELEVEN —

The Program Before School

Friday morning, Astra opens her eyes and stares into her dark room. She rolls over and turns her alarm off five minutes before it's set to ring. She glances at the curtain covering the window and realizes the morning sun has yet to awake.

Feeling her eyes shooting with electricity, Astra lets out a big grin as a different morning lies ahead. With a racing heart, she kicks the sheets and large blankets off herself and onto the floor. And, in one smooth motion, she bounces up from her bed and lands on her feet. Taking a moment to stretch, she hears several joints crack as they wake up from their *own* rest. She bolts out of her bedroom and into the bathroom.

Getting ready for the day, Astra dashes between her room and the bathroom. Eventually, she stops and stays in her room to switch out her pajamas for her school attire. She spins in front of a mirror and lets out a cheerful grin. Afterward, Astra grabs her backpack and races out of her bedroom. Rushing into the dining room, she drops her bag by her feet and sits at the table.

☆ ☆ ☆ ☆

Meanwhile, like every other day, Astro wakes up to his ringing alarm — though earlier than usual. He shuts it off and lays in his bed for another minute. Eventually, Astro rolls out of bed and begins his morning routine. Hearing Astra's frantic footsteps outside his bedroom, he spends most of his time preparing in his room.

Strangely, opposite of Astra — and his usual nervous demeanor — Astro isn't fazed about leaving early. Instead, Astro appears calm. Oddly calm. The way he gets when he feels himself closing in on solving a mystery, and today isn't any different.

After completing his morning routine, Astro grabs his backpack and exits his bedroom. Joining everyone in the dining room, he sits at the table beside Astra.

They indulge in several eggs, a few slices of bacon, a small fruit bowl, and a glass of apple juice. Afterward, they hop into their car and leave for the before-school program.

Arriving a few minutes past seven, they navigate the school hallways before entering the gymnasium through the main entrance.

The Seeker siblings stop and stand near the entrance. Mr. and Mrs. Seeker continue walking to meet with one of the staff members. The twins slowly scan the gym to familiarize themselves with their surroundings.

	Second Entrance
	Storage
	Main Entrance

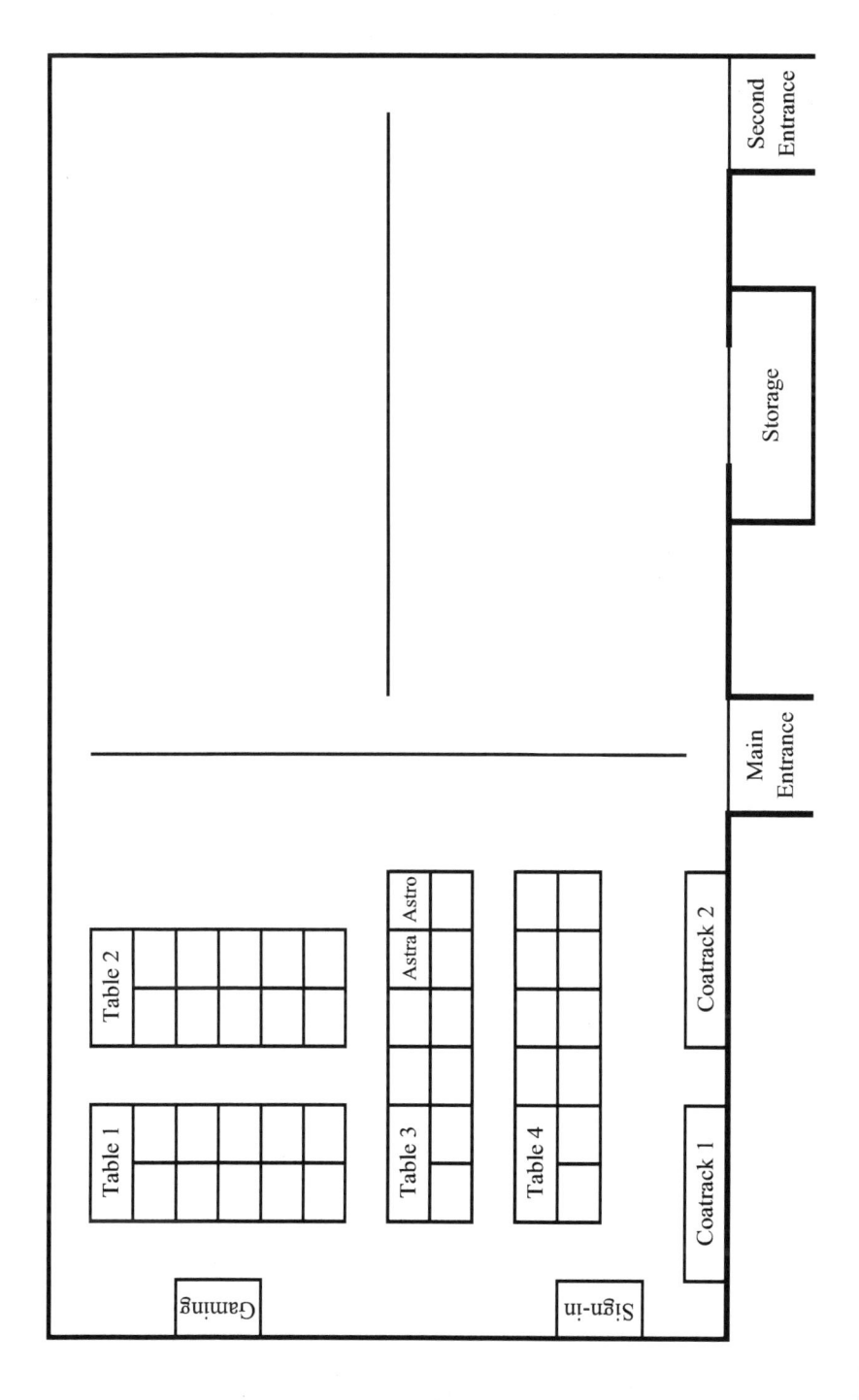

Table 2
Table 1
Astra | Astro
Table 3
Table 4
Coatrack 2
Coatrack 1
Gaming
Sign-in

They notice that the right side of the gymnasium is bare — like during gym class — and focus on the left side.

Cranking their heads to the left, they stare at the two large collapsible coatracks. Close by, a small sign-in table is set up with a clipboard and a pen. Panning right, the twins notice several brown tables — identical to ones in the cafeteria — with games, puzzles, and activities spread out on each one. Near the far-left corner, they see a sturdy AV cart with several shelves and a cabinet. A television sits on the top shelf. Beneath it, on the second shelf, is a gaming system inside a hard plastic case.

Mr. and Mrs. Seeker pass the black coatracks and rejoin their children near the entrance.

"Okay," Mr. Seeker says, "you're all set!"

"Be safe and have fun," adds Mrs. Seeker, quickly kissing their foreheads.

Hugging their parents and saying their goodbyes, Astro and Astra watch their parents walk back through the doorway and exit the gym.

Turning around, they're left alone with a few other early arrivals and several staff members.

Sauntering to the furthest coatrack, the twins hang up their bags on the metal hooks. Astro grabs his special notebook. Turning away, they see a frail old lady hobbling over. With each step she takes, the lanyard around her neck swings back and forth.

Tracking it with their eyes, they read the ID badge and look at the picture of the woman — which must've been taken *several* years ago.

A few feet away from the Seeker siblings, the short lady hacks into her hand. "Morning, kiddos," she greets with a shaky, hoarse voice. "You can call me Judy. It sounds like it's your first time here." Judy turns her head and coughs into her hand. "Feel free to play with any of the activities. Or, if you want, you can join us for some arts and crafts."

Astro watches Astra's eyes light up as she steps forward.

"Ooh, wow! It all looks so nice!" compliments Astra, covering up Astro's dull response. "I'm Astra! This is my brother, Astro. Thank you for inviting us. But I think we'll look around for now. But don't let us stop you!"

Judy coughs again before responding, "Sounds good. You're welcome to join at any time." She hobbles to the

★ THE SEEKER SIBLINGS ★

table closest to the coatracks and starts her daily arts and crafts project with a few students.

Astro and Astra wander around the left side of the gym. After a couple minutes, they sit across from each other at one of the tables.

"Astra," says Astro, tapping the bench beside him. "Why don't you come sit next to me."

"Yeah?" Astra grins and gets up from the bench. "If that's what you want." She walks around the end of the table, switches sides, and sits beside her brother.

Astro wipes the tabletop with his hand to make sure it's a clean, dry surface. He places his notebook down. As they wait for their friends, Astra brings over various puzzles and games.

Twenty minutes after seven, they see Jack and Anna stroll through the entrance. The Seeker siblings watch as they walk to the coatracks, hang up their backpacks, and turn away.

Astra stands up and stretches her neck as high as she can to make herself more visible. Making eye contact with Anna, she smiles and waves.

"BESTIE!" Anna yells from across the gym.

★ THE SIBLINGS' DOUBLE TROUBLES ★

Rushing over to join the Seeker siblings, Jack and Anna sit together on the opposite side of the table. Anna sits across from Astra, and Jack sits across from Astro.

"What are you two doing here?" Anna asks, glancing between her friends. "Oh!" — tossing her hair back — "I still have my necklace!"

"Wait!" Astra exclaims. "It looks different!"

"Heh-heh-heh. I see you've got an eye for detail," she compliments. "I've made a few adjustments to make it more like my gold one. Instead of all the colors, my parents and I went and bought these cute gold paperclips. Oh my gosh! You should've seen their faces when they saw me wearing the paperclips around my neck."

Astra giggles and teases, "You mean they didn't *love* it?"

Continuing to laugh, Anna says, "They were so confused! Oh! These pieces are a little smaller, so I added a few more clips."

Astra squints and looks at the necklace closer. "OH MY GOSH!" she hollers, lightly smacking the tabletop. "THERE'S A TINY HEART IN THE PAPERCLIPS!" She shakes her head and looks at her brother. "Sorry, Astro! But this one's *way* cuter than yours."

Anna adds, "This one's a little longer, but I think it's closer to the length of the gold one." She looks at Astro. "Whatever it takes, right?"

Astro grins and nods. "Whatever it takes."

"But seriously!" says Jack. "What are you two doing here?"

Astro bounces his eyebrows and grins. "Why, we're here to solve a mystery."

"Yeah!" Astra says before ducking and softening her voice to a whisper. "Like *detectives.* Like *secret* detectives. Like the *best* secret detectives! Er-like the best, *double,* secret detectives! Like the —"

"Jack!" interrupts Astro. "Mind if I see your homework?"

"Oh, uh, yeah! Okay," he says, swinging his legs out from the end of the table to get up.

He runs to his hanging backpack. Unzipping it, Jack sticks his hand into his bag and grabs his math worksheet — tucked inside the left pocket of his folder. He zips his bag shut and rushes back to the table.

Handing it off, he copies Astra's exaggerated British accent from the other day and says, "Here you are, good sir."

Astra grins and nods at him in contentment.

★ THE SIBLINGS' DOUBLE TROUBLES ★

Dropping his jaw and raising an eyebrow, Astro stares at them in disbelief as they try to keep from laughing. "Uh-huh," he grunts with a tiny grin.

Glancing over the homework, Astro begins checking the answers.

"Hey!" Astra says, getting up from her seat and walking around Astro. "Since it's our first time here, will you two show us around?"

"Oh my gosh! Yes, bestie!" Anna accepts, getting up from her seat and linking arms with Astra. "Gah! I can't believe you're here right now! I'm so pumped!"

"Pumped?" Astra raises an eyebrow. "*How* pumped? Like water balloon or floatie?"

"MM, I'm thinking . . . bouncy house!" Anna giggles.

Astra's grins at Anna's witty response. "Oo, I'm so sorry, bestie. The *correct* answer was car tire!" she teases with a wink.

Jack stands and joins them as they walk to a nearby table. "We have to hurry, though! Breakfast is in a few minutes!" he warns.

Seeing everyone rushing and leaving the table, Astro places the worksheet inside his notebook — between the cover and the first page. Guaranteeing its safety, he gets up with his notebook and joins his friends.

Walking around and stopping by the different tables, Jack and Anna rush through explanations of the various items and activities.

"Oh!" gasps Jack, bolting to the television and gaming console. "Did you see this? This is definitely one of the best things here! Not to brag, but I'm way too good at one of their dancing games."

Astra grins. "So you got the moves for the grooves?"

Jack shakes his head from side to side. "No, no, no, no, no, no! I definitely do *not!* Games are different than dancing," he says, walking back from his humble brag.

Astra holds a wink and raises an eyebrow. "Uh-huh, *suurre,*" she teases with a skeptical expression.

Astro stares at the table nearby. "W-What's all this about?" he asks, nodding at a line of students sitting behind the person playing on the console.

"Ah. So basically, depending on the game, the person playing gets a few minutes, or a round, before the next person in line gets to go. But if we fight, a staff member will come over."

Astro squints and turns his head to the side. "Uh, okay?"

Jack chuckles a few times. "Oh, sorry. I forgot that it's your first time here. If someone comes over, they'll send everyone fighting to the back of the line. And if that doesn't work, or there's whining, they'll take the console away."

Astro raises his eyebrows. "OH! *Now* I see," he says with a grin. "That sounds strict. But it looks like you've got a good system."

Jack exhales. "Tsh, yeah! You got that right. But if it's just one person causing problems, they'll only punish them. So, most of the time, it works. They *have* taken it away before, though. So they're not bluffing," he adds.

"What happens then? What do *they* do?"

"Mostly sulk," Anna chips in with a disturbed face. "It's awkward . . . for *everyone.* They all wander around the gym like zombies. Doing nothing with mopey faces."

"That sounds painful," admits Astra, peeking at the clock — protected by a metal wire guard — hanging above the gym's main entrance. "Hey, wait. What time did you need to leave for breakfast?"

Jack looks up at the clock. "AH! Anna! It's seven-thirty! We gotta get in line!" he shouts, heading toward the entrance.

"Wait!" Astro yells, grabbing the worksheet from inside his notebook. "Back in the folder!"

★ THE SEEKER SIBLINGS ★

"Right!" Jack snatches the homework and sprints to his backpack. He stuffs his math worksheet inside his folder, zips his bag shut, and hops into the line forming near the entrance.

Anna shakes her head, watching Jack frantically run around. "I don't know how his head is still attached," she comments with a subtle grin.

Astro squints. "Uh, because it's connected —"

"No, Astro!" Astra interrupts.

Anna giggles. "Are you two coming to breakfast?"

"No," Astro says frankly before remembering Astra's reply from her earlier conversation with Judy. "B-But thank you for inviting us."

"Aw-oh. Really? A-Are you sure?" she asks, hoping to change their minds.

Astra smiles. "Don't worry, bestie! We're not going anywhere! Go! Go!"

Anna sees part of the line leaving. "Okay," she says, nodding and grinning. "We'll be back at like eight!"

Astro and Astra watch Anna sprint to the entrance and join the end of the line as it exits the gym.

On the way back to their table, Astro grabs a pencil off one of the tables. They sit in the same seats.

★ THE SIBLINGS' DOUBLE TROUBLES ★

Astro leans toward Astra's ear and whispers, "Please watch for anyone that walks up to the coatrack."

"Okay. Anyone specifically?"

He tilts his head down and stares at Astra with a dead gaze. "Anyone looking suspicious. Anyone hanging around the coatrack. Anyone opening more than one backpack. Anyone steal —"

"*Okay, okay. I got it.* It was a silly question."

"And don't stare too much," he adds, opening his notebook. "Just act like we're drawing or something."

With a pirate voice, she says, "Aye," — pointing to her eye — "aye, Capt'n!"

Astro grins, and they pretend to play a game in his notebook while keeping an eye on the coatrack.

Fifteen minutes pass with nothing appearing out of the ordinary.

With the time literally ticking away, Astro's right leg begins bouncing. He starts tapping the pencil's eraser on the tabletop. Shifting his gaze between the clock and the coatracks, Astro bites the inside of his bottom lip.

Feeling the bench bounce, Astra furrows her eyebrows and shifts her focus from the coatracks to Astro.

Sensing Astro's nervousness slowly overtaking him, Astra's heart begins pounding. Feeling uneasy from taking on Astro's nerves, her breathing turns shallow, and her stomach aches. She closes her eyes and takes several slow, deep breaths.

After calming her emotions, Astra slowly slides her hand across the tabletop. She gently places it on top of Astro's and feels his hand twitch as he continues to try to tap the pencil. But after a few seconds, Astro's hand relaxes. Soon after, the bouncing bench stills.

Feeling Astra's presence with him, Astro takes some deep breaths of his own. His nerves begin to subside as he continues staring at the coatracks, the clock, and the entrance.

With the time hitting seven-fifty, the Seeker siblings see a tall, broad-shouldered student stomp through the main entrance and into the gym. With a grumpy, crabby expression, he marches toward the coatracks. The boy stops directly beside Jack's backpack and drops his bag on the ground.

Astra nudges Astro's arm and whispers, "Astro."

"I see him," he whispers back. "Don't stare, but I bet he checks his surroundings."

On cue, the brooding boy glances over his shoulder while removing his coat. Using his large jacket, the boy covers Jack's bag. Then he lifts his backpack off the floor

★ THE SIBLINGS' DOUBLE TROUBLES ★

and hangs it beside Jack's. The boy stands by the hanging backpacks and coats, disappearing amongst the heap of items. After a minute of fidgeting with his materials, he moves his backpack and jacket to another location. The boy speedwalks away from the coatracks to join his friends at the table near the television and gaming console.

"I bet he just took it," Astro whispers, tracking him with his eyes.

"Really?" Astra stands. "Then we should —"

"No!" Astro shouts accidentally before lowering his voice back to a whisper. "If we do something, we're just going to cause chaos. Jack needs to handle this with his parents and Ms. White. Okay?" He sees Astra continuing to stare and hold her ground. "Agreed?"

Astra clenches her jaw and glares at the boy and his group.

Astro hesitantly reaches for Astra's hand and lightly holds a few fingers. "Astra . . . please."

Gritting her teeth and squeezing Astro's hand, Astra grumbles. "BOOO!" She slowly sits back down and releases Astro's hand. "But agreed."

After collecting themselves, the Seeker siblings turn back to the coatracks and continue watching over Jack's backpack. There are a few additional arrivals, and some students put away their arts and crafts projects, but no one goes near Jack's bag.

Several minutes before eight, Astro and Astra watch a staff member with curly brown hair get up from one of the tables. She's a tall woman with a slight hunch that makes it appear as if she's always leaning forward. They watch her walk to the unused side of the gym.

The woman removes the lanyard from her neck and uses one of the keys to unlock the storage room. Several seconds after stepping inside, she reappears with a large mesh bag filled with colorful foam dodgeballs. Dragging it across the gym, she watches a group of students gather and join her at the middle line. She releases the black clasp, holding the bag shut, and pours the balls onto the floor. They bounce and roll in every direction.

The students quickly jump in and help gather all the loose balls, lining them up on the center line.

As the clock strikes eight, the Seeker siblings hear shouting outside the gym. Turning toward the entrance, Astro and Astra watch the students return from breakfast. Jack and Anna are the first ones to sprint back into the gymnasium.

— CHAPTER TWELVE —

Two Truths and a Lie

Jack and Anna sprint and rejoin Astro and Astra at the table. But before anyone can say anything, Astro holds his hands up and stares straight into Jack's eyes.

With a stern voice, Astro says, "Will you please go check your bag for your homework?"

Jack turns back and looks at the clock. "Oh, sure. But it's earlier than yesterday," he comments before jogging off to his backpack.

Anna peeks at the right side of the gym. "Looks like dodgeball! What do you say?" she asks with a toothy smile.

Astra pounces up from her seat. "Of course!" She looks down at her brother. "Astro?"

"I think I'll just watch this time," he says with a nod.

The girls run to the other side of the gym and join the dodgeball group — splitting into two teams.

★ THE SEEKER SIBLINGS ★

Jack returns, slightly out of breath. "It's not there! But" — pointing to the dodgeball group — "I'm gonna go play! Did you want —"

"No, no! Go!" he says, waving him off. "But can I go and double-check your —"

"Sure," he spits out before dashing off and joining the girls.

With his friends preparing for dodgeball, Astro looks around and checks his surroundings. *Looks like everyone's distracted,* he thinks. *And there's no time like the present.* Astro stands and grabs his notebook.

Astro discreetly ambles to the coatrack and opens Jack's backpack. Peeking inside, he locates his friend's school folder. He reaches in, spreads it open, and flips through the papers. He sighs and removes his hand from Jack's bag. *Yeah, it's really gone,* he thinks. Soon after, he zips it shut and walks to his own backpack. He places his notebook inside his bag and strolls away from the coatracks.

On his way back to his seat, Astro notices the two teams lining up on opposite sides. To his left, he finds Astra, Anna, and Jack. He sits down on the bench and turns his head to the right. He spots the student from the coatrack and several of his friends.

★ THE SIBLINGS' DOUBLE TROUBLES ★

Tweet-tweet! A whistle blows, and the sound echoes throughout the gym.

Students from both sides sprint to the center line toward the dodgeballs — patiently waiting to be thrown at people.

The bully and his friends target a few of the weaker players. Then, they start picking off the younger players. Eventually, Jack gets hit in the chest by a ball. He drops his shoulders and hangs his head. Jack walks to the sideline, exiting the game.

Astro watches Jack lean against the wall on the other side of the gym. With a gentle smile, he gives a subtle wave.

Jack lifts his head, smiles, and waves back. Afterward, he turns his attention back to the game.

Astro does the same, and they watch Astra and Anna continue to play.

The girls work together to slowly pick off the other players on the opposite team. They throw, pass, catch, block, and dodge.

As the game continues, Astra starts sensing Anna's frustration with her wildly bouncing necklace. She sees Anna instinctively reaching up to adjust it after each of her movements.

"UGH!" Anna growls, running and getting a foam ball. She grits her teeth, slaps the ball, and waits for her friend.

Astra retrieves a blue ball from nearby and stares at the coatrack bully on the opposite team. "Oh-ho-ho-ho-ho," she deviously chuckles under her breath. Rejoining her friend, they nod at each other and throw their balls simultaneously.

Anna's ball smacks the wall on the other side. "Man! Seriously?" she groans, upset with herself.

Astra's ball hits the bully's left leg.

"COME ON!" hollers the bully, staring at Astra. "Are you for *real* right now?" He shakes his head, grumbles, and sulks on his way to the sideline.

Astra smiles back at him with a cheeky grin. *Ohhh-yeaaah! Now that . . . that felt good,* she thinks, holding back a content laugh. *Yeah. Jack was so right. That was definitely thunderstorm-worthy.*

Anna focuses on the opposing team as they scramble to retrieve balls. She retreats backward to the wall behind her. Lost in the game, Anna begins reaching up to the back of her neck with her hands. She unclasps her paperclip necklace.

★ THE SIBLINGS' DOUBLE TROUBLES ★

Out of the corner of her eye, Astra sees Anna removing her necklace. She slowly widens her eyes and drops her jaw, forgetting about the dodgeball game.

At the same time, Astro lifts himself from the bench and raises his eyebrows. Both of the Seeker siblings' eyes lock onto the paperclip necklace.

With fire-blazing eyes, Anna continues focusing on her opponents. In a competitive trance, she drops her necklace behind her. It lands by the wall, near a group of roll-away volleyball poles stored in the corner.

As the paperclip necklace hits the ground, the girls get hit simultaneously. Anna drops her shoulders, and her arms dangle limply as she watches the bully and his friends cheer and celebrate.

On the other hand, Astra forms fists and throws them above her head. "YEESS!" she yells, confusing the 'winning' team.

Everyone in the gym stops and stares for a second before continuing their activities.

Snapping out of her trance, Anna shoots her friend a confused look. "Bestie?"

Astra puts her arms down. "ANNA! Do you realize what you've done?"

"Huh? What! What'd I do?"

★ THE SEEKER SIBLINGS ★

"Bestie! Where's your necklace?"

"It's right" — feeling around her neck — "here. Here. Here?" Anna widens her eyes.

"No! It's there!" she yells, pointing behind her at the small pile of paperclips. "You dropped it by the wall and volleyball poles!"

"W-What? B-B-But," Anna stammers, dropping her jaw in disbelief.

Walking over to her necklace, she notices the four volleyball poles sitting on their circular bases in the corner — arranged in a two-by-two grid.

Bending down and picking up her paperclip necklace, a tiny glimmer catches her eye.

Anna furrows her eyebrows and crouches beside the volleyball poles. She leans over and peers into the space at the bottom — formed by the four circular bases.

"NO WAY!" she squeals, jamming her fingers into the small diamond-like hole.

Anna slowly lifts her hand out of the space. Between her thumb and index finger is a dusty gold chain. Holding it by the clasp, "Anna" dangles before her eyes. Tears begin flowing down her cheeks as her gold necklace sways in the air.

★ THE SIBLINGS' DOUBLE TROUBLES ★

"ANNA!" Jack shouts. "YOU FOUND IT!" He sprints to his sister.

In starstruck amazement, Astra whips her head back at Astro — who's standing and watching near his seat — and smiles. But realizing he might not understand, she runs over and wraps him in her arms.

"Good job, bro," Astra compliments. "You've done it again."

Astro smiles and returns her hug.

As they release each other, Astra sees Jack and Anna heading toward them. However, Astro peeks around the gym and notices people staring at them. His eyes widen, and his blood runs cold.

"L-Let's sit down, please," Astro suggests with a cold sweat, lowering himself back onto the bench.

Astra sits on the bench beside him.

With a snotty, crackly voice, Anna calls out, "Astra! Astro! I —"

Astra presses her finger against her lips, reminding her friend to keep quiet.

Reaching the table, Anna sniffles and says, "I-I don't know what to say! Thank you *so much* for your help! I never would've found it without you two." She places the paperclip necklace on the table and starts putting on her gold necklace. "Wait. You two were waiting for me to set it down, weren't you?"

Astro and Astra smile before Astro says, "I'm sure someone would have found it eventuall —"

"No way!" Anna cuts off, drying her eyes. "This one's all because of you two!"

Astra nods. "Thanks, bestie," she says, accepting the compliment.

Anna pumps her fist in the air and whispers, "The Seeker siblings shoot again!" Everyone's faces contort as they flash her looks of confusion. "L-Like shooting stars. A-And you know" — beginning to blush — "y-your names!"

"Ohhh," everyone sounds at once.

Astra giggles, trying to save her friend from dying of embarrassment. "That's a cute one, bestie! I'll have to remember it!"

Jack clears his throat. "I hate to ask . . . but have you figured out what's been happening to my —"

"Question," Astro interrupts. "What's" — tilting his head toward the coatrack bully — "*his* name?"

They follow his gesture and see the coatrack bully playing in the second dodgeball game.

"Ohh," groans Anna. "That's Jack."

★ THE SIBLINGS' DOUBLE TROUBLES ★

"WHAT?" Astra shouts before covering her mouth.

Astro raises his eyebrows and drops his jaw but remains silent.

Jack winces and adds, "Yeah. You might've guessed, but he's the leader of that scary group I mentioned."

"I don't think I've seen him before," Astro says. "He's not in *our* class, is he?"

Jack shakes his head. "Nah, he's in another fifth-grade class. It sucks that he shares *my name*," he says, forming a playful smirk. "He's making us *other* Jacks look bad! Givin' Jacks a bad name everywhere!" He lifts his fist in the air. "That's what I say!"

Astra covers her face and giggles through her nose.

Astro grins, raises an eyebrow, and glances between Jack and Astra. "Riiight. Well, we believe he's the one that's been taking and using your homework."

"What! How do you know?" Jack questions. "Using my homework? Like a copy and dump?"

Astro scrunches his nose. "A what? Listen. After you two left for breakfast, we sat and watched over your backpack. Jack —"

"Not you, Jack. Bully Jack," Astra clarifies.

"Right. He was the only person to go near it. Then, when you came back and checked for it, it was gone,"

Astro answers before squinting and furrowing his eyebrows. "I-I don't know this 'c-copy and dump' thing, but I don't think so. I think he is literally *using* your homework. Since you two share a name, he can take it and say it's *his* homework."

Jack drops his shoulders and slumps over, putting his left cheek on the table. "S-So what do I do now? It's not like I can just tell him to stop. Th-That's *way* too scary."

Astro nods. "Mh, yeah. *I* would suggest telling your parents. Then they can call Ms. White or something."

"And if you need any help, we're here," Astra adds. "But it might be better if *you two* explain the situation."

Jack lifts his head and rests his elbows on the table. "Jeez! I can't believe it," he says, placing his chin in his hands and furrowing his eyebrows. "But why didn't he take my reading homework too?"

Astro thinks for a few moments before his eyes light up. "Maybe because it's a packet!"

Everyone squints in confusion.

"W-What do you mean?" Jack asks.

"Quick, go get your reading packets!" Astro instructs. He looks down at the tabletop and grins. "And you can put your paperclips away."

★ THE SIBLINGS' DOUBLE TROUBLES ★

Anna smiles, and they pop up from their seats. A minute later, they return and drop their reading packets on the tabletop in front of Astro and Astra.

The Seeker twins stare at their packets of half-sized sheets of paper — enough for the entire month.

Astro's heart pounds as he reaches for Jack's packet. "Let's say you filled out one of your reading summaries for the month," he starts, pointing at his packet. "Then, the next day" — sliding the packet in front of Astra — "bully Jack takes it. You would get a new one, right?"

"Right," Jack answers, seeing Astro reach over and slide Anna's reading packet in front of him.

"Okay. That night, you go home and fill out another reading summary in your new reading log. The next day, he steals your packet again, right?"

"Right," he repeats, watching Astro slide the second packet in front of Astra.

"That means he'd have two reading packets with one summary in each. But that wouldn't make any sense."

"Ohhh," everyone sounds simultaneously.

Jack furrows his eyebrows. "Wait a second. Couldn't he copy the reading summary into one packet?"

"Maybe. But again, that's risky. That's *especially* true now that we know Jack's stealing your homework *at school*."

Everyone nods in agreement.

"But I still don't understand," says Jack. "Out of all things, why steal my math homework?"

Astro nibbles on the inside of his lip before guessing, "For appearances?"

"Huh? What do you mean?"

Astro exhales. "If someone doesn't have their homework, it's easy to believe they're not smart."

Jack stares at the tabletop and reflects on his missing homework experience. "I mean . . . yeah," he agrees.

"But if you *always* have it," continues Astro, "everyone might start believing you're intelligent."

Jack's eyebrows twitch as he continues to stare at the tabletop. "Wait. Since I didn't have *my* homework, does that mean —"

"Of course not!" Anna cuts off in a defensive tone. "You always try your hardest, and that's what matters! So don't you ever think less of yourself!"

Astro and Astra simultaneously widen their eyes and stare at each other.

Jack gulps and nervously smiles at his sister.

★ THE SIBLINGS' DOUBLE TROUBLES ★

"Honestly," says Astro, "the only thing not smart is stealing someone else's homework. He should've tried his best instead of becoming a thief."

"Aw, now I feel bad for him," Astra says with a tiny frown.

Astro's eyes turn desolate, and he shrugs. "Well, he shouldn't steal other people's work," he criticizes coldly.

Astra grimaces, knowing everything isn't always so black and white. Raising an eyebrow, she peeks at Astro out of the corner of her eye and asks, "Why haven't you made a machine to measure hard work yet? You could even add a place to enter everyone's situations!"

Astro scoffs. "*Yeah, right. That* type of thing sounds impossible," he replies with a smug smirk before realizing the point of Astra's comment and gulping.

In fact, Astra unknowingly gets into Jack and Anna's heads as well — softening all their hearts in the process.

"Wait," Anna says, interrupting the sudden silence. "You two solved both of these mysteries by yourselves? How?"

Astro and Astra widen their eyes.

"Oh-ah-er-um . . . l-l-luck?" Astro answers, using the first excuse that enters his head.

Jack and Anna exchange doubtful looks before going along with his answer.

Astra's face turns red, knowing they didn't buy that for a second. But abiding by Astro's wishes, she protects their secret and doesn't say anything.

Astro narrows his eyes and glances between Jack and Anna with a piercing expression. "Please . . . don't forget our deal," Astro says sternly. "Don't go telling people that we helped solve either of your mysteries, okay?"

Jack and Anna nod, promising to keep their end of the agreement.

Astro takes a deep breath, softens his intense gaze, and relaxes.

At eight-thirty, the staff releases everyone from the gym. The two pairs of twins exit the gym with the rest of the students. They stroll through the halls and into Ms. White's classroom together. For the first time since meeting, the Seeker siblings observe their friends without the weight of black holes weighing them down.

— CHAPTER THIRTEEN —

Friends and Families

With such an abnormal start to their entire day, the Seeker siblings enjoy the familiarity of sitting in their assigned seats. The school day slowly begins to feel like their usual routine. However, and for good reason, Jack and Anna are in spectacularly good moods.

During the morning meeting, Jack and Anna have enough excitement and energy to charge a solar panel. But as Ms. White releases everyone back to their seats, Jack's vibrancy vanishes.

Jack sulks and drags his feet across the floor as he dawdles to his desk. Lifting the top of his desk open, Jack finds his school folder and slides his hand through the top. Feeling around, he locates his reading log by its unique size. Jack grabs it, closes his desk, and drops it on the surface. Flipping through, he finds his latest reading entry and waits in his seat.

Seeing Ms. White closing in with her clipboard of judgment, his heart sinks and threatens to fall through the floor.

Approaching Jack, Ms. White begins writing on the paper snapped into her clipboard. "Reading, no math?" she predicts.

Jack turtles his head and tries to hide. "R-Right."

With disappointment painted across her face, Ms. White shakes her head and lets out a heavy sigh. "Once again, next week is a new wee —"

"Jack!" Astro cuts in, shifting their attention. His palms sweat as he stares into Ms. White's eyes, keeping Jack in his peripheral vision. Using a stern tone, he asks, "A-Are you *sure* you don't have your math homework. You didn't even look."

"Really, Astro?" Jack complains. He holds his reading packet, opens his desk, and grabs his folder. Setting it on his desk, he notices several classmates staring — including Anna and Astra — and turns red.

"Really," Astro answers, still staring at their teacher.

He whips his folder open. "You, of all people, should know" — hopelessly shuffling through the papers — "that it's . . . it's right . . . here?"

★ THE SIBLINGS' DOUBLE TROUBLES ★

Ms. White snaps her head down, losing her staring contest with Astro.

Inside his folder, tucked behind the first few papers, is *his* math homework, with *his* name written at the top, in *his* handwriting.

A faint smile spreads across Astro's face as Ms. White stares at Jack's math worksheet.

Ms. White raises her eyebrows and smiles. "Wow! Yeah, it looks good — great! It looks great!" she praises, changing her entry. Staring and squinting at Astro, she asks, "Is this a new Jack?"

"Y-Yes?" Jack answers, copying his teacher and looking at Astro.

The classmates nearby join Jack and Ms. White in their shock and confusion. But Astro's too busy staring at Ms. White to notice.

Even though Ms. White accepted Jack's homework, she glances at Astro several more times as she checks the following students.

Continuing to maintain eye contact with Ms. White, Astro grins and yawns. Afterward, she stops looking and resumes her homework check.

Jack acts as if his math worksheet is an award or certificate. With a goofy grin, he slides his worksheet back

★ THE SEEKER SIBLINGS ★

into his folder. He opens his desk and slides his folder inside.

After closing his desk, Jack leans over and whispers, "Astro, how —"

"Sh," he hushes without moving his face, still cautious of the teacher.

"But —"

"Sh, later."

Jack nods and stops pushing for an explanation.

Ms. White finishes the homework check and starts the class schedule.

The morning disappears faster today, or so it seems. Whether it's the mysteries, the fact that it's Friday, or the fun activities, the four find recess appearing quicker than usual. But *as usual,* they all head to the swing set.

"Jack!" Anna shouts. "How did you have your —"

"I-I-I don't know!" he responds as they walk across the multicolored pebbles to the swings.

Astro locates an available swing and sits down with his notebook. He places it in his lap. The others stand in front of him instead of taking the adjacent swings. They all stare with eager expressions.

Astro lightly smacks his lips, creating a tiny popping sound. "Maybe I should explain. I, uh" — coughing into

★ THE SIBLINGS' DOUBLE TROUBLES ★

his fist and clearing his throat — "I-I made a copy of the math homework."

Astra shakes her head in confusion. "What? More details, please."

"B-Before completing my math homework, I made a copy of it. Then, I filled in the answers on both worksheets. On *my* sheet, I, of course, put *my* name. But on the copied version, I put *Jack's* name."

"Wait, what?" Jack says, dropping his shoulders. "So the worksheet in my folder isn't actually *my* worksheet. It's your cop —"

"No! That *is* your worksheet!" Astro stresses.

"But you said —"

"I *said* I filled out the answers and put your name on it. But think back to earlier this morning, right before breakfast. I told you to put your worksheet back inside your folder," Astro says. "Now tell me . . . how close did you look at the worksheet? Did you actually stick *your* homework into your bag? Or did you stick something *else* in there?"

"Huh? W-Well, I put what you gave —"

"Oh my gosh!" Anna shouts excitedly. "You never returned his homework! You gave him *your* version! THE COPY!"

★ THE SEEKER SIBLINGS ★

Jack snaps his head back and forth between Astro and Anna. "WHAT? Wait, wait, wait, wait, wait. Wait! I never even *saw* another worksheet! How did you switch them without —"

"With this," Astro interrupts, holding up his hard-covered notebook. He flips the cover open and explains, "I hid the copy here. Then, while you two were giving us a tour, I switched them."

Anna looks at Astra. "Wait. But weren't *you* the one who asked us to show you around? So does that mean you were in on this —"

"No way! I honestly had no clue! I mean, I *did* notice he stopped by our family computer space. But I didn't think he actually *did* anything!"

Jack drops his jaw and rapidly walks in tiny circles with his hands on his head. "Okay, wait!" He stops and looks at Astro. "When? *When* did you have time to put mine back?"

Astro smirks. "Ah. After breakfast, I asked you to check your bag for your homework. You came back and said it was gone. Then *I asked* if I could double-check." He nods and bounces his eyebrows.

Jack gasps. "You weren't double-checking! You were putting my worksheet back!" he shouts. "Oh my gosh!

★ THE SIBLINGS' DOUBLE TROUBLES ★

What am I hearing right now? Am I awake? Someone slap me! I'm dreaming!"

Astra smiles and walks over. "Okay! Better get ready tho —"

"No! NO!" he declines, laughing. "Not for real!"

Astra giggles and steps back. "Ack, dang."

"Wait a second," Anna says, "you said you filled out answers on both worksheets. So bully Jack still gets a worksheet, doesn't he?"

Trying his best to hold back a smirk, Astro purses his lips. "Y-Yeah, sure. Well, kind of. I-I may or may not have filled it out with a bunch of random numbers. And on the back" — beginning to chuckle — "I may or may not have drawn random symbols and hieroglyphics!" Astro bursts into cracks of laughter.

All at once, Astra, Anna, and Jack close their eyes and sigh through their noses.

"Ohh, Astro . . ." groans Astra. "Only *you* would find that funny."

Astro continues laughing, making the swing chains rattle. After a minute, he holds his side. "Ow, ow, ow!" he yelps, laughing in pain and wiping his tears. "Thank goodness the other Jack took it too. I would've felt bad if our Jack had to show Ms. White the crazy hieroglyphics homework." Astro lifts his voice as high as he can and says, "Awkward."

They all laugh with Astro before hopping onto the adjacent swings.

After recess, Jack and Anna shine for the rest of the school day. In fact, they're so bright that their infectious attitudes rub off on their surroundings. However, when the school day ends, Jack and Anna still remain distant. They don't talk to one another on the bus, on the walk home, or as they enter their house.

Anna slips her shoes off first and heads toward her room.

Still fidgeting with his second shoe, Jack realizes he isn't going to get his shoe off before she disappears. Jack stands up and shouts, "ANNA!"

Anna stops at the entrance of the hallway and spins around on her heels. "Hmm?"

Feeling his palms sweat, Jack gulps and takes a deep breath. "W-Would, ah — w-would you want to... watch a movie? And, um, like, y-you know, do homework?"

Anna gasps, and her eyes light up. "R-Really? Yeah! Okay!" she accepts, changing directions and rushing into the living room.

Jack smiles and breathes again. "I-I'll be right there!" he shouts, bending down to finish untying his shoe. "I'll grab us some orange juice!" He rushes to the kitchen.

"Yay! I'll get a movie ready!"

Jack and Anna eat snacks, do homework, and watch a movie together for the first time in weeks.

An hour into the movie, Anna looks at her brother and whispers, "J-Jack?"

Jack grabs the remote and pauses the movie. "Hm? Yeah?"

Hearing the sudden silence, Anna widens her eyes. "I, uh. I-I-I," she stutters before taking a deep breath. "I'm sorry for accusing you of stealing my necklace. I was just so mad, and sad, and everything." She releases a deep, regretful sigh. "But I should've believed you when you said you didn't take it."

"N-No, that's okay. I'm also sorry. I shouldn't have said you were taking my homework. I thought you were trying to make me look bad," Jack explains, dropping his shoulders. "But I should've trusted that you wouldn't do that." Jack takes a guilty gulp. "M-Maybe we should try working together next time?"

"Yeah," she agrees with a subtle smile. "I'd like that."

With silence filling the air, Anna recalls a comment Astra made when they first met and starts thinking to herself. *Should I tell him? I mean ... is it that important? He probably already knows.* She looks over at Jack, and he smiles. She gives a faint smile and looks away. *Ooh, what do I do? I can't just randomly tell him. It would be too weird. And I doubt he even thinks about this type of thing. No! Stop making excuses. I should tell him anyways.*

After a few moments, Anna looks back at Jack. With a quivering voice, she says, "Y-Y'know, Jack. I'm always going to be there for you." She turns her head to avoid eye contact.

Jack's eyes widen, and he finds himself out of breath. With watery eyes and a shaky voice, he says, "I-I'll be here for you too, sis."

Feeling small tears in her eyes, she looks up at the ceiling. Anna quickly points to the television, and Jack resumes the movie.

As soon as their parents arrive home, Jack and Anna team up to explain Jack's homework situation.

Jack and Anna's parents nearly die of shock from what they hear — their children working together. Even though they're angry that someone's stealing their

★ THE SIBLINGS' DOUBLE TROUBLES ★

son's homework, they're more relieved to see Jack and Anna in their loving and friendly nature. Not only that, but they're also ecstatic to see and hear about Anna's gold necklace.

Their mother smiles and asks, "So, how did you two figure all this out?"

Jack and Anna widen their eyes and freeze. But after locking eyes with each other, they grin and nod before answering, "With luck."

Seeing their parents exchange confused and doubtful expressions, Jack and Anna giggle.

Over the weekend, Jack and Anna's parents believe they're hallucinating as their children get along better than they have in a long time.

☆ ☆ ☆ ☆

That afternoon, something similar takes place in the Seeker household. Astro and Astra complete their usual after-school routine and finish their homework assignments. Afterward, they pack it away, and Astro retrieves his notebook. He begins filling in the results of the two mysteries.

★ THE SEEKER SIBLINGS ★

Astra stands up from the couch and stretches. "Want me to grab you a snack?"

"Sure! Will you get me a banana?"

Astra heads to the kitchen and looks on the counter. "Ahhh-no!" she yells. "It looks like they're all gone!"

"Oh. I think there should be two fruit cups in the fridge."

Astra walks over, opens the fridge, and looks inside. "Hmm, I only see one!"

Astro furrows his eyebrows, looks up from his notebook, and stares straight ahead. "Mm, do we have any pudding cups?"

"We do!"

He relaxes his face. "Phew!" He looks back down and starts writing again. "Okay, I'll have one of those."

She grabs it and returns to the living room, handing him the pudding cup with a spoon. "Sorry! Maybe Mom or Dad will go shopping this weekend."

Astro smiles. "Yeah! It's never good when we run out of snacks," he agrees, peeling off the film and taking a bite of his pudding.

Astra takes a bite of fruit from the remaining fruit cup. "So Astro? How'd it feel to solve another mystery? No! *Two!* Another *two* mysteries!"

Astro tilts his head left and right, mimicking a windshield wiper. "Mm, I guess it was alright. How did it feel for —"

"Yeah, right. You loved it!" Astra emphasizes. "Don't even try and deny it."

"Well-I. Er-uh. MM," sputters Astro. "It was good to help out. But I *still* think we jumped into the mysteries too soon."

"*Mh-hmm.* Well, *I* had fun," she says with a grin. "It's just like riding a bicycle!" Astra frowns. "Too bad it's not like riding a tricycle." She looks at Astro. "Get it? Because a tricycle is easier to ride than a —"

"Yeah, yeah," Astro interrupts with a faint smirk. He takes another bite of pudding before expressing, "Well, it *was fun* doing the cases with *you.* We make a pretty good team."

Astra completes a double-take before turning away and blushing. "Y-Yeah," she agrees with a soft, timid smile. "We do."

Unbeknownst to Astro, Astra will be replaying his comment for as long and as clear as she can.

As the Seeker siblings finish their movie and snacks, the siblings' double trouble mystery comes to an end. Even so, Astro and Astra make two new friends in their new classroom, at their new school, in their new town, in their new state.

A Seeker Siblings Memory Game

Let's test that memory!

As you may have remembered, Astro's memory isn't the best. Luckily, he has his notebook to help!

But how good is your memory? How much do you remember about the mystery? Try answering the questions below! Do your best!

What color are the Seeker siblings' eyes? _____

What colors are the Seeker siblings' hair? _____

What row is Ms. White's class
assigned to in the lunchroom? _____

Between which two times
does Jack's homework vanish? _____

Who greets the Seeker siblings
at the before-school program? _____

What shape is in Anna's updated necklace? _____

What drink does Jack bring Anna? _____

What snacks do Astro
and Astra eat at the end? _____

Dear reader,

Thank you for bringing the Seeker siblings into your lives and joining them on their first mystery! Be on the lookout for the second mystery in "The Seeker Siblings" series.

<u>If you enjoyed the book, please feel free to leave a review! And make sure to share with your friends and family!</u>

Additional Information (2023):

If you'd like to reach out to the author, you can try the following:

- Email: Author.andrewpowers@gmail.com

If you'd like to learn more, receive updates, and join the author's journey, feel free to check the following:

- Facebook: facebook.com/author.andrewpowers
- YouTube: youtube.com/@author.andrewpowers

Made in the USA
Columbia, SC
04 June 2025